BITTER

"Lord forgive me for my Sins"

Dina Smiley

Try and try again it's never easy being a boss. Soar bravely over life's obstacles not everything you lose is a loss

Copyright © 2019 Shadina Garner
All Rights Reserved
Dinasmiley1@gmail.com

Thanks for the support hope you enjoy!

CHAPTER 1 (The lingering animosity that follows an apology) to be full of anger, hurt and resentment due to one's bad experience {**BITTER**}

"Come here sweetie I got you" an unknown voice said as she picked Diamond up from the floor. Where's your mommy? Are you all alone? She asked

Diamond rubbed her eyes trying to make sense of what's going on "Mommy" she cried looking around

"Where is your mommy? Is this your house?" the unknown lady asked again knocking on the door Diamond was laying in front of.

"Hello is anyone here; your baby is out here! Hello" she yelled banging on the door not getting any answer. It was 9 degrees outside, and 2 yr. old Diamond was in the hallway of Bryn Mawr projects with just a diaper on. She had dried tears on her face and her pamper was full of urine. Her condition showed she had been out there for some time now. "I'm calling the police" the lady yelled again as she pulled out her phone looking up and down the hallways, but no one was in sight.

"911 what's your emergency"

"Hello, my name is Michelle Grimier I'm at 342 Dusky St Apt 5! Yes the Bryn Mawr High-rise. I was coming into the building going to my apartment and there was a little girl in the hall half naked and freezing. No one is answering the door of the house she was sleep in front of

I banged several times! Can you send a car ambulance or something please?"

"Yes, Ma'am I'll send a unit over right away

"Thank you" she said before hanging up.

"Come with me sweetie let's get you warm she said as she wrapped up Diamond in her North face bubble coat wrapping her scarf around her head. Diamond shivered as she tried to suck up as much warmth as she could. The police arrived 7 minutes later, the two officers tried to bang on the door again but there was still no answer.

"Is anyone home the police officer yelled" as he heard a smash of glass break inside the home. Michelle shrugged her shoulders as she held on to Diamond to keep her warm. The officer kicked the door open as him and his partner entered the home.

"Hello, is anyone here, it's the Youngstown Police" One of the officers yelled with his gun out in front of him as his partner followed. The two entered the living room where they found Cynthia Waters Diamonds mother lying on the couch with her throat slit ear to ear as she dangled off the couch head first. The window leading to the fire escape was smashed. "It looks like the prep took the escape out of here. Sick bastard must've thought he was doing a good dead putting the baby in the hall alone in this weather to avoid seeing her mother like this." He said to his partner

"Dispatch, we got a DOA and we need to get victims advocate over here" the cop radioed

Michelle stood outside confused as to what could have possibly happen but knew it wasn't looking good especially for the baby she had in her arms. She dread the sight of what she probably witnessed in her short time of life.

"Ma'am victims advocate will be here momentarily to take the baby"

"Did I hear you say DOA? Is that young girl her mother?" Michelle asked worried

"Yes, ma'am I'm afraid so! Did you notice anything out of the ordinary or see anyone coming or going when you found the baby?"

"No, I was going to my apartment and the baby was lying in the hallway sleep shivering, I tried to knock but there was no answer. I see a few people come and go but nothing that caught my attention to panic. I see this baby quite often and she's usually happy and dressed. This is terrible! What will happen to her?"

"As of now were going to get her checked out make sure she's ok then try to contact some family hopefully there's someone to take her if not we'll find a nice home for her to go to. Here comes the advocate now." The cop pointed

"Hello Guys, hello ma'am I'm Laura Victims Advocate. I'll be taking her would you happen to know her name?"

"I'm sorry I don't but she's very scared and very cold" Michelle said as she handed over Diamond to Laura.

Diamond took one last long look at Michelle as she was carried out of the building still wrapped in her coat.

"Okay honey let's get you out this coat and into this nice warm blanket" Laura said taking the coat off Diamond. She realized what she was doing and began to cry kicking her feet and holding on to the coat with all the strength she had left.

"Okay we can keep the coat on" she said as she held her in her arms

After Diamond was cleared from the hospital Laura took her to the police station for the night. She got her nice and comfortable, got her some warm milk and sat with her until she fell asleep. After laying Diamond down she turned on the 11ocklock news.

Breaking News: {**Cynthia Waters 19 from Bryn Mawr High Rise was found murdered in her apartment this evening**}. As a picture of the little girl and her mother looking so happy flashed across the screen {there are no suspects at the time, but we have her little girl in our custody. If anyone is related or has any idea of who we can contact about her, please come forward with any information. Thank You}. Laura stared at the picture and then back at the sleeping baby wondering to herself how she still does the job she does. After the entire scene the baby witnessed tonight, she still slept so peaceful. Laura pulled up the chair next to her and closed her eyes.

The next day Diamond opened her eyes to a very unfamiliar place. Still wrapped in Michelle's coat she sat up and noticed Laura sleeping in a chair next to her.

"My mommy" she cried. Laura was woken by her voice

"Hi sweet girl" she smiled back

"My Mommy" she cried as she looked around for her mother. Laura picked her up with such a heavy heart trying to sooth her.

"Mommy go bye bye but were going to find you a great home and hopefully a new mommy ok baby" she said as rubbed her head bouncing her up and down

"Garson!" the detective yelled grabbing Laura's attention; we got someone here to identify the baby!

Laura peeked out the door and stood a tall chocolate man with a baldhead and a big beard looking like he was in his mid-40s. His eyes were light grey, but the baby favored him.

"Ok you stay here I'll be right back Laura said to Diamond. Laura walked to the front desk. Hello, I'm advocate Garson how can I help you?"

"Yes, I'm here to pick up the baby that was on the news last night her mother was murdered in Bryn Mawr she's my granddaughter."

"Can I see some identification "Laura asked, the tall dark man reached into his wallet

"My name is Elliot Waters he said showing his ID. The woman you found last night is Cynthia Waters here are her pictures she's my daughter and that little girl is Diamond Waters she's my granddaughter. We haven't spoken in almost 3 years when I found out she was pregnant we had a big disagreement and I made her leave my house and haven't spoken to her since. I always kept tabs on her, and I can't say I agreed with how she was living. I'm going to hate myself forever for that, but I be damned if my grandbaby goes into the white man's system.

"Ok Sir please have a seat while I get some confirmations, I'll be right back "Laura went into the back where she ran Elliott through the database, and everything corroborated with his story. She took the information to the Sgt and was given permission to release Diamond to her grandfather.

"Ok Sir, it looks like everything checked out give me a second I'll get her things together and bring her right out." Laura gathered up all her things and picked her up to hug her "Hi Diamond! Is your name Diamond? We have someone here to give you a nice home ok sweetie lets go meet him." She said carrying Diamond out to her grandfather. Elliot stood up to greet the baby with such ease on his face. This was his first-time seeing Diamond and was so amazed at how much she resembled her mother. The two stood staring at each other for about a minute before Diamond reached out and tugged on his beard as they both smiled.

"Good luck to you sir, she's a fighter to be so young. Things are going to be a little tough adjusting to at first, but you make the best home you possibly can for this baby ok." Laura said walking them out

"Yes, Ma'am will do, Elliot said before exiting the precinct." Let's go home and meet your auntie and cousins and get you a nice room to sleep in"

5 weeks later

Knock knock knock

"Who's there" Elliott yelled

"Bam" he replied

Elliott got up to walk to the door "Yes how can I help you?" Bam removed his hat

"Hello Sir, I'm not sure if u seen me at the funeral but I was really good friends with Cyn (Cynthia)" Diamond was running around playing when she heard a familiar voice in the door way. She ran in between her grandfather yelling "BAM BAM BAM BAM" running into his arms

"Hey pretty girl Bam replied picking her up smiling

"Are you her father?" Elliot asked confused

"Uh no sir can I come in please, so we can talk" Elliott moved to open the door for him to enter and guided him to the living room. Bam walked in still smiling so happy to see Diamond and. Diamond smiled so happy to see a familiar face after so long, she wouldn't let him put her down. "Let me call my daughter to come take her so we can talk. "Hey Mercedes! Elliott yelled come get Diamond, so I can talk to this young man

"Coming she replied"

"This is Mercedes, Cynthia little sister, Cedes this is Bam a friend of your sisters!

"Yea I remember you. Any friend of hers is a friend of mine" Mercedes said extending her hand to shake not taking her eyes off him.

"Nice to meet you Bam said handing her Diamond

"Come here lil mama" Mercedes said grabbing Diamond and taking her up the steps

"So young man what would you like to talk about" Elliot said

"Well sir like I was saying I was good friends with your daughter before she passed, and I love Diamond like she's my own, it's terrible what happen to Cyn I don't understand it honestly. She told me she was playing with the white girl heavy so I think it caught up with her, but I didn't know she was that…

"Excuse me young man but the white girl I'm not familiar with this term!" Elliot responded

"My bad I mean drugs sir, she found someone that helped her make money since she was on her own with no help. I told her it was dangerous, but she said she was protected! Now my baby is out here by herself."

"But I thought you said she wasn't yours" Elliott ask in confusion

"No sir she's not, wait you don't know what happen to her?" Elliot's eyebrows rose.

"Sir she was raped by 2 masked men one night after being drugged at a party! She had no idea who Diamonds father was. Shit she had no idea she was pregnant until it was too late". Elliot couldn't believe his ears. "You made her leave sir and she had nothing or no one. I helped her deliver Diamond on the steps of Bryn Mawr and have had a bond with her ever since. That's what I mean by my baby."

"I had no idea" Elliot replied in tears

"I don't mean to upset you, but I need you to know the full story. She was a good girl until then and she hated you for thinking anything different! But that's the past I'm here to ask you if it's ok if I continue to see Diamond. She's my heart and no offense but I need her as much as she needs me. She doesn't have a father and now no mother she has you all, but I love her too."

"As you see I'm getting old now, I then took on this baby with the help of my daughter of course and it's been hard these past 5 1/2 weeks but I'm dealing with it. I know this is going to take some time for her to get used to so patience is of virtue but since she's been here, I haven't seen her that happy until she seen you so I would be honored if you can remain in her life. I know I didn't do right by my Cynthia but I'm going to make sure I can do everything I can to make Diamond as happy as I most possibly can."

"Thank you, sir, he smiled Can I see her?

"Sure! Diamond he yelled, Mercedes carried Diamond back down the steps staring at Bam with lust in her eyes.

"Girl hand him over the baby that's his god daughter" Mercedes smiled and handed her over

"Can I get you something to drink?" Elliot asked

"Sure" Bam replied

Elliott walked into the kitchen to get Bam a drink while Mercedes sat and watched Bam playing with Diamond.

"So, Bam what's your story handsome, I see you looking at my peach you want a taste"

Bam gave her the look of death "Look shorty no disrespect but I didn't come over here to entertain your hoe ass so let me handle my B.I then I'm out your way. Go take a cold fucking shower and pipe down. I already know about how you move" He expressed showing off his nine in his coat with a sneaky grin on his face. Her eyes got big as he put his finger to her lips "SHHHHHH don't start nothing won't be nothing now take your ass upstairs I'll see you again real soon"

Mercedes got up and ran upstairs while Bam waited for his drink holding Diamond on his lap

"I got a present for you" he said pulling two Q Tips out of his pocket…"Baby girl open wide say awww"

"Awww" Diamond said opening her mouth as Bam swabbed the inside of her cheeks

"Good Girl, he said kissing her forehead

"Alright, I thought I had a better variety of drinks, but it looks like you're going have to settle for this Strawberry Fanta that's all we got" Elliot said laughing

"Sir I appreciate it, but I actually got to go forgot I got to pick up my pap from the VA hospital at 2 but it was a pleasure and you will be seeing a lot more of me I promise and this lil one too aint that right baby girl" Bam said

"You're leaving already! Ok well if you have to but come back you hear" Elliot said

"Bye Bye Bam Bam" Diamond waved

"Definitely you'll see me real soon, he said walking to his car. (Beep beep) he waved pulling off. Pulling out his phone: **DONE** the text read as he hit the send button

CHAPTER 2 (Easy on the eyes yet disguising on the heart) There's reality that sets in just not the way one wants, when it fails do you sink or swim {**HARSH**}

"Babe you got mail" Mika screamed walking back in the house.

"Bring it here I'm bagging up bae" he replied

Mika walked up the steps into the attic where the air was flooded with heroin dust "Here boy you know my skin gets irritated from this shit, she said handing him the mail and running back down the stairs. She handed him 2 envelopes 1 reading LabCorp... Bam's eyes grew big and his stomach began to flutter with nervousness as he opened it.

Dear Bernard McKinley,

This letter is to inform you of the results from the genetic testing conducted in your DNA package that consisted of a collection of swabs for two individuals. The test report show that you are NOT the father of the child (ren) for whom the test was conducted as follows:

99.99%, meaning pursuant to the stipulation entered in this matter, that you are conclusively determined to NOT be the father of such child (ren). Attached is the original report and results to keep on file for your records.

If you have any questions, please feel free to call toll free 1800 454 3454

Thank you

{Bam help me please, please help me} the screams replayed over and over in his head

Bam sat on the bed relieved but upset at the results. He loved Diamond like his own but knew there was no way he could explain how he was her father without admitting to hurting her mother. That also meant he knew exactly who her father was. They haven't talked or seen each other since that dreadful night he still has nightmares about and Bam wanted to keep it that way. Visions of her lifeless body haunted his dreams and kept him up most nights. He felt responsible for all the hurt she endured all the way up to the night she was killed. If she would've never got pregnant Elliot wouldn't have kicked her out. If she wouldn't have gotten kicked out, which lead to her murder? He didn't feel like he was a rapist and spent every day afterwards trying to make it up to her and now Diamond.

Bam picked up his phone "Yo" a male voice answered

"What up Nig we need to catch up got to rap to you" Bam said

"Oh, now niggaz got rap! I aint heard from you in a minute what I owe the pleasure pussy boy"

"Nigga and you know why but don't think I aint been keeping tabs on you boy. Aint sweating it though this bigger than that"

"No nigga it aint so don't flatter yourself! You see what I want you to see so don't forget that. You can sit up there acting all mighty but guess what you the same nigga as me partna don't forget that"

"Beast I'll never ever compare myself to a scum ball ass clown like you. You know what fuck it I'll see you around" Bam yelled before hanging up the phone.

"Babe everything ok" Mika yelled

"Yea babe, can you get Druzy on the horn and tell him I said 0 percent grove in 30, he'll know what I mean" he replied throwing on his Steeler Hoodie and Timberlands

Bam gathered the 60 bricks and headed out. The sun was shining bright in Youngstown and everybody was out enjoying the day but Bam felt like there was a black cloud over his head. Deep down he really wanted to be Diamonds dad. He walked around with such a heavy heart knowing what he knew about her mother's death and smiling in Diamonds face like everything was ok.

Bam pulled up to the grove where Druzy stood smoking his blunt.

"Damn nigga you shining boy" Druzy said approaching Bam's car

"Ha ha you know a lil something I do this" Bam responded

"Yeah I see you man, so what u got for me"

"Before we get started I reached out to Cyn's dad just to see if they had any evidence witnesses anything and it looks like shits cool on your end, as fucked up as that shit was" he said shaking his head

"The bitch couldn't play her cards right," Druzy responded nonchalantly

"Man, you aint have to do her like that though damn"

"Hey all about my money your done! Besides ya man Beast did the dirty work. I'm sure you remember since you were there, I just gave the order!" Druzy said putting out his blunt "I mean you got a problem with the way I work?"

Even though Bam had so much animosity towards Druzy he knew not to bite the hand that feed him.

"What! He laughed it off, Man listen its M.O.E money over everything you know that! Fuck all this bullshit let's get down to the B.I" Bam replied pulling the duffle bag out the car. Everything's straight as usual 1 up 2 downs we rolling so I guess I'll see you in a week.

"Roger that brotha you be safe out here" Druzy said before hopping in the car.

♪All thru the hood I keep hearing niggaz saying "IM GONNA DIE TONIGHT" ♪

Bam sang to the music as he drove the streets of North heights smoking his blunt. He pulled up to the red light where he spotted Mercedes coming out of DeLuca's Pizza. "Damn all that ass in that skirt, too bad I can't touch it! Ya poison!" Bam yelled out the window pulling up to the pizza shop.

"What nigga! How about don't say anything to me with your crazy ass" she replied before getting in her Camaro.

"Nice car you must suck a mean dick if you pushing that niggaz whip"

"Oh, you know my nigga; good I can't wait to tell him how disrespectful you are so he can deal with you accordingly"

"Don't flatter yourself ma", he said grabbing the door before she could shut it. Ya nigga aint built like that and trust me he don't want them type of problems and neither do you. I just need you to past on a message to Beast for me!

"Yea and what's that!"

"Just because the apple didn't fall far don't make it ok to taste! He dead wrong for that he'll know what I mean"

"Is that all" she yelled Bam let go of the door and blew her a kiss before letting her pull off. Mercedes had no idea what she was getting herself into or that Beast was the unknown father of her niece. She had been dealing with Beast for about 9 months now. They met while she was leaving Charlie's hair salon. He offered her a ride and from that day she been riding ever since. Bam recalled seeing her around town rocking his chain driving his car playing wifey making moves for him. Her father would never approve of him, so she didn't bother to bring him around Elliot to avoid any confrontation.

Mercedes pulled up to the trap house on Lowry Way where Beast was. He had just got a new shipment in and needed to set up shop to get it broke down bagged and distributed. She knew deep down this lifestyle was out of her league, but she loved it at the same time. The money was fast and easy, and she loved spending it.

"Hey baby", she said walking in

"What up what up, he replied

"Do you know some nigga name Bam on some personal shit because he acts like you two was best fucking friends"

"Bam ha-ha he laughed yeah I know that nigga we just got off the phone why what happened"

"He mad disrespectful, I met him awhile ago. He stopped pass the house to see if he could keep seeing my niece apparently him and my sister was good friends or some shit. But I was just trying be nice you know show some hospitality and he snapped the fuck out on me ole weird ass nigga"

"Yea that's Bam, uptight as fuck. You know how niggaz be when they got a chip on they shoulder. And he wasn't just a good friend he was obsessed with your sister"

"Well whatever I just ran into him again and he act like we got beef or something what's his fucking problem he said some shit like don't taste the bad apple that fell from the tree or some shit I don't know I wanted to get away from his weird ass"

Beasts smirk instantly left his face, what exactly did he say? He asked aggressively standing up

"Umm I don't know something about a damn apple and a tree" she responded taking off her shoes

Beast slapped her "bitch think hard" he yelled

Mercedes screamed holding her face looking at Beast with fear in her eyes

"Umm Umm she stuttered ok he said (*Just because the apple didn't fall far don't make it ok to taste*) does that mean something baby I'm sorry she began to cry.

Beast took in what she said "no baby I'm sorry he said kissing her cheek that was bright red from the slap, he's just a swift nigga so when he sends messages there's always some catch or underlined message you have to find that's all. I can't get caught slipping with this nigga! He got too much dirt, how's your face I apologize."

"It's ok" she replied, this isn't the first time he put his hands on her but the apologies always felt like it would be the last time. Beast picked her up and laid her on the table

"Don't cry you know I hate it when you cry, he said kissing her inner thigh. She laid back staring at the ceiling as tears rolled down the side of her face. Deep down she knew this man was toxic, but she couldn't get out. She took pride in being tough enough to take the punches and still stay in the fight. Beast slid her panties the side "You want this dick don't u" he whispered as her pussy pulsated and dripped down her ass. He licked and slurped every drop while Mercedes moaned with her legs spread apart. Beast flipped her over to her stomach and pushed her head down on the table while slowly entering her.

"Oh shit she moaned" as he stroked harder and harder smacking her ass.

"I love this pussy! Is this my pussy?"

"Yes, baby it's all yours,"

"I'm sorry baby, you know I love you I don't mean to hurt you" he whispered before pulling out and Cumming all over her ass. Mercedes laid bent over the table trying to control the shaking in her legs. One thing that Beast knew how to do was take her attitude away. He knew where every sweet spot to g spot was on her body and he touched every one.

"Damn boy, she said fixing her panties" she noticed there was blood in between her legs. She ran into the bathroom to wipe and clots were on the toilet paper.

"Baby she yelled in a panic"

"Yo, he responds"

"We need to go the hospital"

"What for it's a little blood quit being dramatic, he responded walking in to the bathroom, I probably knocked your period out you good ma!"

"No, I'm not! This aint no period babe, hasn't been for about a 2 in a half months" Beast looked at her confused... Baby I took a pregnancy test 3 weeks ago because I was late and it was positive" she said looking down at her feet afraid of his reaction

"3 weeks he yelled why the fuck you just now saying something!"
"I wasn't sure what I wanted to do don't be mad"

"You getting rid of that shit I don't want any fucking kids!" he yelled smacking her in the face again. The smack caused Mercedes to fall off the toilet hitting her head off the tub. Mercedes screamed holding her head and stomach as blood dripped from her head "Get up man, he yelled grabbing her. He noticed the deep gash on her head pouring with blood. "Fuck when we get to this hospital you bet not say shit! If they ask questions you tell these white people no parts of our business you understand!"

"Yes, she cried"

She wrapped a towel around her head as he dragged her to the car. Disappointed she road in silence light headed leering out the window wondering how a man so sweet can turn into such a monster in a matter of minutes. Is this the type of man she wants to create life with, parent with, be involved with she thought? Despite what he said Mercedes was happy about the pregnancy and didn't want to get rid of the baby.

They pulled up to St. Peterson Hospital on the upper Eastside. Beast helped carry her out the car and walked her into the emergency room.

"We need a Doc my girl just took a spill in the bathroom we need help!"

Ok the nurse replied pulling up a wheel chair, what's your name Ms.?

"Mercedes, she replied dazed and confused. They took her to the back while another nurse got more information

"She can't seem to tell us much Sir was she raped I see blood in between her legs?

"Hell no she wasn't raped we was at the spot doing our thing I might have been hitting it to hard and she started bleeding. She went to clean up and fell in the bathroom!

"Ok well we need a little information for registration can you fill this out the best of your knowledge. I'm sorry I didn't get your name Sir.

"I didn't give it either" he responded

"Uh ok she replied clearing her throat, when you're done just take those forms to the front desk. We're going to need you to sit in the waiting room afterwards and we'll keep you informed of her outcome." She said before walking away. Beast looked down at the papers looked out the front door sat down her paperwork and proceeded to walk out the hospital leaving Mercedes alone.

The nurse came out 10 minutes later to inform Beast of Mercedes condition but noticed the paperwork on the table but no sight of Beast. She grabbed the papers and went back into the hospital room Mercedes was in.

"Ms. Waters, the nurse said getting Mercedes attention. I just went out to get your husband, but I couldn't find him anywhere. Maybe he went out for a smoke perhaps!

Mercedes put her head down in shame "he doesn't smoke "she whispered

The nurse looked at her in confusion "don't get upset ma'am we have some great news not only are you pregnant but you're having twins! Mercedes looked up in shock "Twins! What the hell am I going to do with twins" she cried

"You'll be fine sweetie you just got to have faith god will see you threw children are a blessing believe me I have 4 she smiled. Now we're going to keep you here for the night just to run some test. It looks like your blood pressure is a little high so get comfortable alright. Is there anyone that you would like for me to call?

"No ma'am I'll do it myself thank you"

"Alright I leave you to it then, the nurse said exiting the room"

Mercedes picked up her phone to call Beast (Operator voice) ~ *you have reached 3 0 3 4 4 5*~ she hung up and redialed and got the same voicemail message.

"Baby I know this is a surprise for you it's a surprise for me too, but this is our blessing baby. I know we're going to be ok I love you, you love me please come back. I'm here all alone and I really want you here she cried. The nurse even told me were having twins baby 2 little bundles that will look just like they daddy please be as happy as me because I'm not killing them I just can't do th… BEEEPPPPP the voicemail sounded cutting off her voicemail.

Beast pulled up to the Bryn Mawr Projects where Daeon and Mills were parked:

"What Up what you niggaz into, he said getting out the car

"Aint shit trying stack this paper, Daeon responded"

"I heard that! Mills who you boo loving wit on the horn", he joked

"Hold on Stacks, Mills said into the phone. Nigga this is Stacks he said what's up with that move? Mills replied

"Tell him I'm still thinking about it but I got him, matter fact make sure I get his number from you before I dip."

"No doubt Stacks let me rap to this nigga real quick and hit u back in a grip, bet" Mills said before hanging up

Stacks was Druzy's brother and a well-known drug dealer/ strip club owner of the hottest strip club in Pittsburgh called Sugaa's. Stacks was very well informed about how Beast move drugs threw Youngstown and handle business when needed for Druzy with no questions asked so he was eager to get him down to Pittsburgh to work for him. Beast bounced around about the idea but always waved it off because Youngstown was his life and he just couldn't see himself relocating.

"Have you niggaz rap to Bam lately?" Beast asked

"Yea yup he still around, why what's up" Daeon responded

"Man you know that nigga be bugging sending messages thru bitches to me and shit. The nigga is mad intellectual so I don't know where his head at. I guess he still got his skirt in a bunch I don't know" he laughed

"What happened to you niggaz man yall used to be tight? Now he won't even stop if he sees a nigga with you" Mills said

"Over that bitch" Beast yelled

"What! All this over some pussy nigga which one" Mills asked lighting his blunt

"Man Cyn" the two guys got quiet and looked away

"Don't tell me you niggaz in your feelings about the bitch too, that's part of the game. The boss makes orders I do as I'm told! She got caught biting the hand feeding her, so she had to go, aint no love in this shit"

"I feel you, but she was the family though and in front of her baby that's some cold shit" Daeon responded

"Man fuck that orders is orders that's a known fact Bam knew that too when we knocked on her door that night. He knew what I was going in there to do and he didn't stop me cause at the end of the day ORDERS IS ORDERS you niggaz better get your head in the game"

Mills and Daeon got quiet, they couldn't relate to what Beast was saying. Everybody loved Cyn she was such a high-spirited person always there for everyone. She would give you the shirt off her back if you needed it. It was a hard pill for everyone to swallow but business must go on, so everyone went on with life as if nothing ever happened but deep down they were hurt by it.

"I'm out shoot me Stacks number, you niggaz stay up and off that emotional shit get back to this money, Beast said before getting in his car"

While driving his phone went off, it was a text message with Stacks information. He also noticed the voicemail Mercedes left. He listened to it while he scrolled thru the radio stations trying to find a good song barely listening to the voicemail until her heard TWINS. He quickly called Mercedes.

"Hello!"

"BITCH DID I HEAR YOU SAY TWINS

"Yea babe isn't that great news! Don't be mad baby I love you this is good news"

"The nurse said u had a miscarriage"

"No, they thought it was from the bleeding, but everything is fine, where are you I don't want to be alone can you come by"

"Listen here I don't want them fucking kids, what u think we going be some happy family the fucking Cosby's or some shit nah GET FUCKIN RID OF THEM ASAP.

"Please don't do this babe; I'm not killing my babies not for you or anyone ELSE"

"Ok so basically you are saying we done! You're one stupid bitch rule #1 aint no love in the game good luck being a single mom bitch" he yelled as he hung up turned his music up and sped off.

CHAPTER 3 (Not solid firm or genuine in the eyes of someone on the outside) Fraudulent accuracy nonfiction even thru the mask I can see your eyes {**FAKE**}

3 Years ago

"Go Cyn Go Cyn Go Cyn Go Cyn"

"Yo-yo yo I watch him breathe you inhale now ex. don't sweat don't flex or bump up like that shit on ya neck. You rock them Red Monkey jeans like you don't you know that's a test my bees will swarm in ya pocket bitch you gets no respect. And wipe that smirk off ya face I robbed niggaz for less I need an M for some L.E that's what u call fabulous. Oh, you a baller you balling Bam take that chain first you see me now you don't call me the new Dave Blain"

Ohhhhhhhhhhh everybody yelled cheering Cynthia on around the lunch table

"Cyn stop you just killed this man look at his face ha" Daeon laughed along with the rest of the lunchroom. Cynthia and her crew Bam, Teh, and Daeon loved battle rapping at lunch. They never stayed for actual classes, they showed up mostly to floss all their new clothes and shoes sell to their few customers and then they left. Druzy was there boss and he was in the principles pocket, so the crew did what they wanted when they wanted and made money doing it.

"Well you heard the crowd Brink cough up that change nigga"

"Man take this punk ass buck I got plenty baby girl" he said flashing his wade of cash."When you going let me take you out?"

"Nigga step the fuck off" Bam said

"My bad dawg that you "Brink asked insinuating Cynthia was Bam's girl

"No but it aint you either nigga"

"Alright boys break it up let's go we out" Cynthia said

The gang gathered their things and hit the side door. They hung out in the neighborhood projects called Bryn Mawr. That's where all the activity on the Eastside took place and they had it on lock. Anything you needed 1 of the 4 had it. Whether it was weed to pills rock to powder. Cynthia did most of her hustling during the day because she had a strict father who didn't want her doing anything but going to school and coming right back home No boys allowed and no drugs. Her mother passed when she was born so Elliot was a single father of 2 Cynthia and Mercedes. Mercedes was 3 years younger than her and the complete opposite from skin color to body built and brains. Mercedes envied her big sister because she was light skin and popular while she wasn't. Elliott wanted the best for his girls and worked hard to try to give them everything he could, but Cynthia had different plans.

"What up Cyn! What you got for 40 today gorgeous"

"You know I keep the best of the best for you Chop" she responded pulling out an over packed bag of cocaine

"You sure do know how to take care of me baby girl"

"No problem! Don't use it all at once ok Chop" she said embracing him with a hug

"You got it mama"

Cynthia loved the game the hustle and the money, but her heart kept her humble. She hated poisoning her fellow black brothers and sisters, but her motto was "they going get it from somewhere" it worked and she made lots of money.

"Yo Cyn what's up with the what's up P.Y.T when you going let me show you more than these raggedy ass projects you love so much?"

"Neva"

"Damn it's like that" Beast replied standing at 6'4 solid muscle, chocolate as a Hershey with the whitest teeth you'd ever seen

"Yeah you heard me, don't you got enough birds clucking around you anyway? I don't eat birdseeds daddio" she laughed

"Ha birdseeds that's cute, we'll we know you aint taken! You hang with these niggaz every day and I know they aint getting that pussy"

"Fuck you Nigga, what's up with you, Teh said approaching Beast for a handshake

"Aint shit, Druzy sent me over to check up on you niggaz, make sure product moving smoothly you know. I figure while I was here, I try to swerve on Cyn's fine ass again" he said licking his tongue out at her.

"I think not" Cyn responded walking over to Bam. Bam was the closest to Cyn out the crew they were like best friends. What Cyn wasn't aware of was that Bam was in love with her. He loved her since the first time he saw her but valued their friendship so much he kept his feeling to himself.

"Give B a shot Cyn" Bam replied trying to decipher his jealousy

"Boy bye, everybody then had him I'm good! Something about him creep me out its evil in his eyes I don't like"

"Nah he cool peoples but I feel you" Bam said

The 3 stood watching Teh and Beast unload the truck and stocked the walk-in freezer in the maintenance office of the housing project. Druzy always paid the maintenance manager 2000 a month to keep that freezer empty and locked. There were shipments once a month that they broke down bagged and sold to the fiends in the hood.

"You little niggaz going help or stand there all pretty and shit" Beast yelled

Oh, my bad they laughed walking to the Van

Cyn kept checking her watch knowing she had at least an hour before Elliott start searching the streets looking for her. This gave her 45 minutes to finish up go change her clothes and be walking thru that door before he walked out.

"What can I help with Beast?"

"Oh, you want to feel like one of the big boy's nah sexy stay your cute ass on the post we got this" Beast replied closing the trunk

"Yeah aright, well then I'm out guys you all know Elliott about to be on his rampage she laughed

"No Doubt, we'll get at you tomorrow they responded as they walked towards the freezer

"You want me to walk you Bam asked embarrassing her with a hug"

"Boy please its 230 aint nobody worried about my ass but you she responded flirtatiously Bam laughed

"Yea ok well be safe shawty we'll catch up in the a.m.". Beast watched jealously as the 2 flirted. He wanted Cyn bad and couldn't understand why she was the only one he couldn't have.

"Bam is you hitting that? He asked as he watched Cyn walk away"

"No Nigga damn and why you so pressed she aint like that so you might as well pause trying fuck because it aint happening so dead that pimp"

"Damn nigga a lil hostile for somebody that aint had the pussy" Beast said laughing

"Whatever man, Bam said grabbing the last box and walking away.

Cynthia walked in the house at 4:10 just as Elliot was grabbing his coat to go out and find her. Sorry she said the bus had 2 handicap stops you know those take forever"

"Well Mercedes is here! Why weren't you two on the bus together?"

"Daddy now you know we barely see each other in school, and I don't look for her we roll with different groups of people"

"What u mean yall roll? Lil girl that's your sister she comes before any of them nappy headed rag muffins"

"Rag muffins daddy she laughed you're right she said embracing him with a hug Where is she anyway"

"Upstairs doing homework which I'm sure your about to follow correct"

"Yes daddy" she said heading for the upstairs. Mercedes was lying on her bedroom floor doing her homework and snap chatting.

"Umm why the hell are you in my room"

"Please don't you even start be happy I didn't tell daddy that you left school yet again with those drug dealing boyfriends of yours"

"Bitch first of all they aint my boyfriends and don't worry about what the fuck I'm doing because I heard one of those little drug dealing boyfriends of mine caught you trying a jizzle the other day… Wonder if I should tell daddy about that"

Mercedes had a surprised look on her face. "It was one time and I had no idea what I was taking"

"Stop fucking lying! Yeah your lil ass been doing more than that I heard! Oh, you thought I wasn't going find out your name ringing bells. What's wrong with you? You really think these niggaz cares about you?

"You think they care about you" Mercedes snapped back

"I really don't give a fuck, I'm getting money! Enough to get me the fuck out of here No love gain no love lost. While your trifling ass is trying pop your coochie to still be broke. Do what you want I don't give a fuck just stay the fuck out of my room" she yelled dragging her by her arm out the room and slamming the door.

♪Say lil bitch u can't fuck with me if u wanted to these expensive these red bottoms these bloody shoes♪

Blasted the room, while the smell of Youngstown's finest and purest cocaine filled the air. Cynthia took her product home since there wasn't enough time in the day to do it outside the house. Most of her clientele preferred to play with the powder but just recently she picked up a few business men that rather play hardball, so she taught herself how to cook crack an amazed herself because the side rock hustle was a hit. She had already managed to save up 25k. She used a coffee pot brewer to turn the coke into crack and bagged everything up in her walk-in closet labeled with signature smiley faces. When her music was blasting Elliott never bothered her assuming she was doing homework which was always her cover up for prepping for the next day's work.

{Ring Ring}

"Who this"

"What's up this Daeon, you swinging thru tonight I'm throwing a lil gig?"

"No doubt who all coming thru"
"Oh you know it's going be lit I'm bringing the whole city out. How u sneaking out with Pops hawking"
"Nigga now you know me I get around like Tupac" the 2 laughed

"Alright bet! I'll catch you in a minute then"

"Word" she said before hanging up

Elliott works night shift on Thursdays so the party couldn't have been planned for a better night. She danced around her room trying to find an outfit to wear for the night excited to get out of the house. She just bought the new Louis Vuitton platform boots she couldn't wait to show off.

Elliot left about 9pm after checking on both the girls who were already in the bed for the night. He worked as an overnight janitor on Thursdays at UPMC hospital. Cynthia waited about half hour before she snuck out. She crept down the steps so Mercedes wouldn't know she left and snuck out the back door where Bam was waiting to take her to the party.

"Damn girl you look fresh how much them run you?"
"Oh you know a good 1200 hundred she bragged wiping off her boots, you look fresh too what's the crowd looking like you already look lit"

"Ha-ha man I had a couple, it packed already dope bitches in there so you know what I'm fitting to do" Bam said rubbing his hands

The two rode through the streets of downtown Youngstown. The sky was so clear you could see every star. Cynthia closed her eyes and made a wish. Bam starred at her while her eyes were closed. He loved everything about her, her skin was vanilla smooth as silk her lips were so perfect and juicy the way she wore her lip gloss made him melt. He often fantasized about kissing her lips but never had the guts to do so. She was 5'10 with legs for days with the perfect size C Cup titties with a small waist and a round plump booty. When she opened her eyes, she caught Bam steering

"What! What's wrong?"

Bam realized she caught him looking and snapped out it

"I was wondering what your crazy ass was doing I thought u fell asleep" he said jokingly hoping his cover wasn't blown

Cynthia laughed and brushed it off.

Bam pulled up to Teh's house and it was wall to wall packed. Cynthia went straight for the bar

"What's up let me get a Jack &Lime" she yelled

"Jack and Lime what old ass nigga got you drinking that" the bartender replied

"Just pour it" she said

The bartender poured the drink and she threw it back and asked for another one and drank the second just as fast. She looked around and noticed her little sister Mercedes on the dance floor grinding with Beast while his hand was under her skirt.

"Excuse m" Cyn said grabbing her arm. Mercedes looked at her in shock

"Oh, what's up Cyn what u doing here"

"Bitch what the fuck are you doing here and Nigga back the fuck up off my sister

"Sister" Beast laughed

"Yes, Nigga little sister, let's go you're leaving she yelled grabbing her out the room

"No, I'm not leaving I'm having fun you're not supposed to be here either! I'll tell if u make me leave"

"You know what fuck you do what u want bitch I'm washing my hands you want to be grown you got it."

Mercedes walked back over to Beast and Cynthia watched as Beast put the drink to her mouth

"What's up Cyn" Teh yelled catching her in the hallway what's wrong

"Hey what's up, she said not taking her eyes off Beast

"This party is lit though right want to drink" he said dancing in circles around her

Cynthia laughed "You know what that sounds perfect let's hit the bar"

Teh and Cyn took 4 shots and hit the dance floor

♪ Booty me down booty me down shake something girl♪ Cyn grinded her ass all over Teh and he enjoyed every minute of it. Cyn noticed out of the corner of her eye Beast watching her licking his lips as Mercedes danced in front of him "Go Cyn Go Teh the crowd yelled"

"Shit I need to sit down I'm feeling it" she whispered in his ear before finding a seat in the back to cool off.

"Man, what's up with your sister she mean as hell! I never did anything to her, but she acts like she hates my guts" Beast asked.

"I don't know I can't stand that evil bitch either and she can't stand me. She thinks she's so pretty with her light skin and long hair fuck her" Mercedes said

"Damn it's like that she your blood thou"

"So, she always treated me like shit, and everybody always cater to her like she some prize possession. That bitch could die for all I care"

Beast sucked up everything she was spitting out, the evil look in Mercedes eyes he knew he could probably get her to do anything for him. Beast reached in his back pocket and dropped 3 roofies in a drink.

"Aye baby why don't you do me a favor"

"What's that?" she said smiling

"Here, take this drink over to your sister as a peace offering and make sure she drinks it"

Mercedes looked at the drink and could see the fizz from the pill almost fully dissolved (What's it in) she asked

"Do it fucking matter you just said you didn't give a fuck about the bitch"

Mercedes jumped at his assertiveness "I don't I was about to take a sip that's all" she said kissing his neck'

"Nah that will have you on your ass you don't need those problems, now take it over there and make sure she drinks all of it.

Cyn sat fanning herself and wiping the remaining sweat off when Mercedes walked up to her with a puppy dog face trying to gain sympathy

"What the fuck you want" Cynthia said

"Sis I'm sorry, why we got to be like this we're sisters. Cynthia looked at her and rolled her eyes completely ignoring what she was talking about.

"I have a peace offering Mercedes said handing her the drink. I'm sorry big sister" she smiled Cheers Mercedes toasted her cup with Cynthia's and threw the drink back fast Cynthia followed.

"So are we good now?" Mercedes smiled

"We good" Cyn replied walking away

Beast stood across the room watching knowing in just a matter of time the drink would kick in.

"Babe I did I, she ran over laughing she didn't even suspect nothing dumb bitch, I can't wait for my daddy to catch her ass all drunk and shit when she should have been in bed."

"Yea speaking of your daddy I need you to take your ass home it's getting late you know he be lurking the streets and shit"

"Wait but I wanted to spend more time with you he don't get home for another 4 hours" Beast didn't take his eyes off Cynthia as she stood waiting in line to go to the bathroom

"Listen I said take your ass home I'll see you tomorrow, he said pushing her and walking away.

Mercedes caught Beast walking towards where Cynthia stood. "It's always her, no one ever chooses me" she cried leaving the party

"Damn baby you don't look so good you ok, Beast asked knowing that the pill was taking affect let me help you."

"I don't know I feel dizzy or something she said sweating and trying to keep focus"

"Here babe maybe you should lay down come on Teh momma's room is free.

Bam watched as Beast grabbed her hand leading her upstairs. Cynthia could barely keep her balance and her vision got more blurred with each step. Beast picked her up at the top step and carried her into the bedroom and laid her down. Cynthia laid on the bed looking at the ceiling as the room spent in circles before she blacked out. Beast began rubbing on her thighs, he slowly unbuttoned her shirt when Cynthia opened her eyes and tried to push his hands off, but she felt paralyzed. Beast climbed on top of her and slowly undressed her. He kissed her lips and neck as he pulled her perky succulent breast out of the bra cup and gently sucked each one. He licked down her stomach and slowly unzipped her pants noticing that her body was completely lifeless. He pulled her pants down and ripped her panties.

"Stuck up bitch, you aint want to give me no pussy huh now imam take it." Beast pulled down his pants spread open her legs and wiped his dick all over her now exposed vagina. He spit on his hand and smeared it on his fully erected penis and inserted it inside her. He stroked her so hard and rough completely unaware that she was a virgin while her body laid completely still.

"You like that bitch huh, he whispered"

'Yo" knock knock what yall doing in here Bam stumbled in drunk

Bam noticed that Cynthia was passed out and Beast was raping her.

"Nigga what the fuck is you doing" he yelled pushing him off her

"Mind your fucking business she wanted that shit, he yelled pulling his pants up

"How motherfucker she passed out" Bam yelled

"Nigga I know I made sure of that" he smirked get you some I see how you look at her stuck-up ass here's your chance.

Beast walked out the room and went back to the party like nothing happened. Bam covered Cynthia with a blanket and tried to wake her but she didn't budge. He laid down next to her staring at how gorgeous she was even when she slept. One of her breasts was poking out the side of the blanket he tried to cover her with. He couldn't help but touch. He pulled the blanket off her and just stared at her body, he couldn't believe how perfect she was. He knew it was wrong but wanted to know what she felt like just once. His penis was bulging out of his pants and her body was calling him he couldn't resist. He pulled his pants down to his knees and inserted his dick inside her. He went as slow and gentle as possible. He kissed her soft and whispered I love you baby while she laid there completely unconscious. Beast noticed that Bam didn't come back down; he crept back up the steps and peeked into the room.

" Yea I knew you wouldn't pass on that pussy" Beast said watching as Bam slowly stroked her

"Nigga shut the fuck up I'm nothing like you" Bam yelled puling his pants up and covering her

"Nah Lil Bam you're exactly like me" Beast laughed

Bam looked back at Cynthia with such guilt, this was his friend he loved her.

"Man lets go just leave her here and don't fucking touch her. She'll wake up from this and never even know it happened come on man let's just go" Bam yelled pushing Beast out the room. Bam put her clothes back on her and tucked her in the bed kissed her on her cheek and went back to the party feeling disgusted.

Chapter 4 (To rebel for attention that leads to a mistake) constant pokes at the hibernating bear not aware the bears awake {**MALCONTENT**}

Present Day

"Hey I'm here" Bam yelled walking into Elliott's house. Bam has been a huge help when it came to Diamond. She didn't have a want in the world and with Elliott getting older he could use all the help he can get.

"Hey Bam, she's so excited let me grab her coat" Elliott said

"That's not her fucking coat Dad! Mercedes yelled snatching away her daughter's coat. Bam looked at her with the devil in his eyes but kept his comments to himself.

"Okay you don't have to curse, where's her coat at?"

"I don't know she aint my kid" Mercedes responded before walking back up the steps.

Mercedes had a huge chip on her shoulder towards Diamond because she had everything with neither parents while she was stuck with twins by a man who wanted nothing to do with her or her children.

Diamond came running into Bam's arms and his face lit up every time he seen her face.

"Hey baby girl, you ready for your first day of big girl school"

"Yes, but I'm very nervous" Diamond responded Bam laughed

"Nervous! You know if anybody messes with you who going kick, they butt right"

"Uncle Bam Bam"

"Who"

"Uncle Bam Bam" she yelled smiling ear to ear

"That's right" Elliott laughed as he helped gather Diamonds things

"Alright El I'll pick her up too then we'll probably grab something to eat. So, we will be home sometime after 6 that cool with you."

"No problem, have a good day see you later Dime"

Mercedes watched out the upstairs window as Bam put her in the car handing her a new doll, he bought her. She almost hated Diamond even though that was her only niece. When the kids would play together, she would take away any toy that Diamond would pick up that wasn't hers. Sometimes she would even let Kennedy and Kayla team up and fight Diamond and she would just laugh until Elliott came into the room and got them. Mercedes couldn't get a job because she didn't have a sitter, so she was struggling to keep up and Bam made sure that any clothes or shoes that Diamond grew out of he took and threw away before passing them down to her kids. One day while Bam and Diamond were out getting ice cream, she informed him that she didn't think her aunt Cedes liked her very much and it hurt her feelings. So, the next time he seen Mercedes outside the house he put a gun to her head and warned her if she ever did anything to hurt her, he would personally make sure she dies a slow painful death and her kids would be auctioned off to the worst pedophiles ring he could find. From that day forward she just avoids Diamond and forced her children to as well even though there all in the same home.

"Alright let's go school time" Bam said reaching for her hand to walk into the school

Diamond stood with her head down

"What's wrong baby girl?

"I'm scared"

"Scared what I tell you about that word?"

"No one scarier than Bam Bam"

"Ok then you believe me" Diamond looked up at him and nodded her head yes. Bam reached out grabbed her hand and walked her in the school. He never had any children of his own but everyone that sees him around thinks Diamond is his daughter because she had his heart in her back pocket, and everybody knew it and he's never denied it.

"Ok class I want all of you to find the locker with your name on it and put your things inside of it" Ms. Grimier yelled as Bam and Diamond entered the classroom.

"Hello and who may I ask is this?" she smiled referring to Diamond

"Hi this is Diamond Waters she's in this class the paperwork says"

"Yes, I remember her very well I'm Ms. Grimier" Diamond looked up and noticed a familiar face

It was Michelle the woman who found her in the hallway the night her mother died

"How are you pretty girl, you look like you got on with life just fine" she smiled Diamond smiled back not quite sure how she remembers her but felt very safe.

"Bye" she waved to Bam he laughed

"Oh, just like that you kicking me out"

"Ha ha I'm guess she does remember my face are you dad?"

"Not exactly but I'm the closest thing to it, u know her already or something? He asked handing her Diamond book bag.

"Uh kids once you put your things in the lockers take for the introductory game, she yelled. Can I talk to you a sec?" she whispered to Bam. The two walked to her desk,

"I was a real tragedy what happen to her mother, I was the one who found her outside the door that same night. She was so scared she latched on to me and never let go, I know it was years ago, but she gave me the same exact look that assured me she remembered me. But she's in good hands don't you worry."

Bam looked back at Diamond and watched as she sat so pretty and shy, he wanted to stay with her. "Oh yeah I remember them mentioning your name I appreciate you looking out for her she's my lil boo thank you for keeping her safe despite the situation she turned out to be a great kid."

"No problem it's in my nature to take care of the kids as you can see" she laughed

"Cool well I'll get out your way, bye baby girl" he yelled before exiting the classroom.

Diamond watched the other children put their things in their lockers.

"Ok everybody, my name is Ms. Greiner and I will be your teacher for the year helping you guys get smarter and become good friends. So, let's start by going around the room and introduce ourselves. You all know I'm Ms. Grimier and you are?" she said pointing to Diamond. Caught off guard she put her head down.

"It's ok don't be shy," she said walking over to Diamond' but before she could get to her the young man who sat next to Diamond name Jayson leaned over and whispered, I'll go with you ok.

Diamond looked at him nodded and smiled the two both yelled their names

"Jayson Diamond" they laughed

"Well nice to meet you Diamond and Jayson I already know u Jayson you were with us last year!" Come up here Jayson she said... Jayson walked up to the middle of the class. "Ok everyone this is Jayson he was with me last year and will be joining us again this year. The 2 smiled at each other.

Later, that day the kids were dismissed outside for Recess

"Hey Diamond, you want to go play outside with me" Jayson asked

"Yeah ok", she responded

"Ok come catch me" he yelled as he ran as fast as he can to the end of the courtyard where none of the kids were playing. Diamond jokingly ran along chasing Jayson happy she had made a new friend.

Diamond reached the fence where Jayson stood to catch her breath

"You run fast"

"I'm going to be a track star like David Oliver when I get big" he said

"I'm going to be a ballerina when I get big, she responded

"You're pretty can I kiss you"

Diamond instantly tensed up "umm no my uncle Bam said no one should touch me until I'm big"

"Not if you're pretty I touch pretty girls all the time, my little sister like it when I touch her, she's 4 she laughs when I kiss on her private places, she don't got a wee like me. I can kiss your private place if you want."

"No that's nasty, I'm going back in!"

Jayson put his arm around her and locked her in between his body and the fence, come on one kiss he said pressing his body fully up against hers. Diamond looked around but none of the other kids at the end of the courtyard were paying attention. Jayson shoved his hands up her skirt and forcibly kissed her all over her face.

"Stop it! Get off! She tried to push but he was much stronger than her. He managed to get his hand in her underwear but noticed she was crying.

"What's wrong all the girls like it? Diamond tried to push him. Are you going to tell? You better not or I'll have my uncle shoot you!" She pushed one last time as hard as she could causing Jayson to fall to the floor, and she ran away crying.

"Whoa Whoa is everything ok Diamond, Ms. Grimier asked as Diamond tried to catch her breath

"Calm down, breathe" she said, Diamond followed her instructions and caught her breath. Ok now is everything ok did u fall? She asked sounding concerned. Jayson ran over

"Ms. Grimier I accidentally made Diamond fall it wasn't on purpose we were just playing I'm sorry Diamond is your knee ok?" Diamond looked at Mr. Grimier than at Jayson, he had a threatening look on his face as he made the gun sign with his pointer and thumb finger.

"Yes, I'm ok" she said putting her head down

"Ok you sure? Let me look at you she said spinning her around any blood spilling out do I need to get a chainsaw and cut off an arm or something she joked tickling her. Diamond laughed wiping her face.

"Alright guys you've got about 5 more minutes than were going in so have fun she said walking back into the building."

Diamond watched as she walked away, Jayson stood right next to her

"That's was fun can we do it again tomorrow? If you don't, I'll tell my uncle to shoot you in the head I seen his gun he will do it if I tell him"

Diamond walked away from him trying not to cry, he stood watching her as she tried to make friends with the other girls in the playground, but everyone was cliqued up not interested in new friends, so she stood on the wall alone. Diamond watched as the girls laughed and whispered while Jayson played with the boys like nothing happened and it angered her.

The bell rang for dismissal Ms. Grimier dismissed the kids in alphabetical order by their last names Diamond was one of the last kids to be dismissed. Bam was waiting for her at the entrance and her face lit up when she seen him.

"Bam Bam she ran yelling"

"Hey lil mama he yelled embracing her hug" You ok was you crying what's wrong with your eyes

"I hate it here please don't make me go back"

"Why you looked happy when I left what happen, he asked walking her to the car"

"The kids are so mean I don't have any friends"

"But your teacher was nice right
"Yes"

"Baby girl you'll be ok everything is an adjustment remember trust me it will get better"

"Ok I'll go back"

Diamond stared out the window debating if she should tell him about Jayson putting his hand up her skirt, but she got scared that his uncle may shoot her if she told. She decided she would stay far away from him in school from now on.

A couple days went by and Diamond manage to stay far away from Jayson even when he attempted to be nice to her with dandelions; he picked on his way to school. She just ignored him and thought he eventually would have got the point until one day she was walking to the restroom before lunch.

"Hey Diamond" he said pinching her butt

When she noticed it was him, she started walking faster and entered the girl's bathroom. She put her ear to the door to see if he kept walking.

"You can't run forever, he laughed

She stood there for a minute until she didn't hear him anymore then walked into the stall to use the bathroom.

The late bell rung but she took her time using the bathroom to make sure she didn't run into him again. As she flushed the toilet, she heard the door shut. She assumed it was another girl because there was no way a boy would be entering the girl's bathroom. Diamond unlocked the door and Jayson was standing in front of her.

"Hey pretty"

"You're not allowed in the girl's room get out here or I'm going to tell"

Jayson slapped her in the face and pushed her back in the bathroom Diamond cried, you're my girlfriend so act like it he yelled pushing his hands up her skirt.

Diamond froze with tears running down her face while Jayson forced 3 fingers inside her. I love you don't cry it feel good like on TV right he whispered.

Please stop she cried, Jayson stopped and unzipped his pants

2 girls entered the bathroom and scared him, he quickly pulled his pants up and wiped Diamonds tears

"Go out and act like you're washing your hands I don't want to get in trouble for being in here ok don't say nothing Ill sneak out when they leave ok!

Diamond nodded with approval and left the stall to wash her hands. She kept her head down so the girls wouldn't see that she was crying. Both girls looked at her confused

Is u okay? One girl asked Diamond kept her head down

"Umm ok well fuck you too retard" the girl responded laughing before leaving the bathroom.

"I'm going to kill you Diamond cried out, Jayson came out the stall

"But I love you I made you feel good you my girlfriend now"

"I'm going to kill u that's a promise, she said before running out the bathroom"

Diamond went back to her classroom and watched the clock anxious to go home. The teacher tried to get her to participate but she just kept a blank stare at the clock until the bell rang.

Bam waited outside for Diamond to be dismissed when his phone rang

"What's the deal?"

"My money is the fucking deal Ream" Bam yelled

"Nah that's where you're wrong that's my money, I said I needed 10 girls you only got me 7 do7 sound lie 10" Ream replied blowing smoke

"You slime ball motherfucker I promise you, you going have much bigger problems if you don't cut my check nigga. It was 9 remedial ass fuck nigga those was your sloppy ass niggaz that let the bitches OD I don't give a fuck bout none of that! Trust me you going see me" Bam yelled hanging up

He jumped out the car just in time to catch Diamond walking to the car

"Hey Doll baby was this day any better?"

"Yup everything was great I had so much fun" she lied embracing him

'See I told you" he smiled opening her door

"Could I hang with you today, I don't want to go home yet?"

"Sure, let me just let Elliot know" he said texting Elliott

Bam pulled off, so what u want to do today it's your day"

Can you take me to where you and my mom grew up at?

Sure, I'll take you past, but we can't get out of this car it's a little dangerous for you. I noticed you've been having a lot of questions about your Mom lately.

I don't know anything about her or my dad I see everyone else with their parents and I can't really explain anything about mine and you were the closest to my mom so I figured you can show me some stuff maybe even tell me something about my dad.

Bam paused for a second "I didn't know who your dad was we weren't close around that time, but I can tell you some things about Cyn though k" he smiled

"Okay"

Diamond and Bam drove around the Bryn Mawr projects, he pointed out all the different places that him and Cynthia used to hang out he even bragged about how good she was at rapping. Diamond just cruised with a face full of satisfaction. She didn't know much about her mother but the little that she did brought so much joy to her heart. Yet so much pain to Bam's because deep down he knew the tragedy behind her death and the truth about Beast her father.

Alright love that's about it but I got another idea I'm going make a quick stop and then me and you going to go get us something to eat you cool with that

Yup she replied smiling ear-to-ear let's get Seafood

Seafood huh well let's fatten you up and get you all you can eat seafood how about that!

"Yay" Diamond smiled

"What's up OG" Bam said pulling up to the corner store

"Oh, what's up Bam? Who this you bringing them younger and younger I see, what's your name beautiful" Juice said leaning into the car?

"Don't fucking talk to her! Bam yelled Diamond looked afraid. It's ok baby girl he said getting out the car. Come this way get the fuck away from her' Bam yelled

"I'm just playing with your man you never know though she looks so sweet and untouched ha-ha" he laughed

"Nigga say anything else about her your momma going be picking out a dress for your funeral" Bam whispered showing his gun

"We good man relax, he said putting his arms up chill my nephew in their"

"I don't give a fuck get back to the business what up with that north side chain is everything in place?"

"Yeah the phones got turned on yesterday, so the buyers are setting up now"

"Good Good, I might need something else done too but ill drop that info when needed the clock is still ticking on that" A basketball rolled out of the store and a boy ran out after it

"Bam this my ill nephew Jayson, Jay this Bam"

"What's up man, Jayson said reaching his hand out"

"What's up youngin" he responded Diamond caught a glimpse and realized it was Jayson from school. He heart began beating fast.

"Bam can we go now she yelled catching Jayson's attention he smiled and walked over to the car "Hey Diamond", Jayson said smiling

Diamond looked away ignoring him

"You good baby girl Bam asked

"I want to go" she said

"Ok, we can go" he replied looking concerned

"Look man follow up make sure everything is everything for the pick later be back around 9 got me" Bam said to Juice

"Bet on it now Jay lets go boy"

Jayson didn't take his eyes off Diamond "See you at school Monday" he said before running back in the store. Bam got in the car and pulled off. Diamond starred out the window with a completely different mood.

"Ready for some seafood'
"Sure"

"What's wrong Diamond everything ok"

"Bam Bam why you got a gun"

"Well sometimes you need them for protection" he replied

"From who bad guys like Jayson and his uncle"

"Well not Jayson he still a young buck but his uncle yea you never know"

"But Jayson is a bad guy"

"Why you say that Dime"

"I see him around school he's mean to everyone all the time"

"Well you just stay away from him because if he's ever means to you then you know Bam will have to kick his little ass right" he laughed

"Right, she responded can I stay the weekend with you

"Sure you can. I got some running around to do so you may have to sit with Mika for a little bit while I run out but yea if u want.

"Yay, let's get seafood

"Bet" he said high fiving her

Chapter 5 (Pure innocence with disappointments can easily become hostile) Strains and sights of you compare to poison in one's veins. Venom and bad intentions never dissolve it only remains **{VITRIOLIC}**

Sunday Morning

"Tick tock nigga its 8 o'clock bitches to slave money to be made" Juice said entering Bam's bedroom

"Nigga, he yelled pointing his gun how the hell you get in here?"

"Man relax and put that shit down your bitch let me in did u forgot about our 9 o'clock with Druzy? You know he trip when he got to wait on us and shit"

Bam looked at the clock shit aright bet let me hop in this water give me 15 minutes he said throwing his gun on the bed. Juice sat down and grabbed the remote to flick through the channels as he waited.

"Nigga take your ass downstairs baby girl in the back room still sleep don't want you waking her up or scaring her with your ugly ass"

The 2 laughed as Bam excited the room. Juice waited until Bam was completely out of sight. He stood up as if he was about to exit the room but instead walked into the back room where Diamond was still asleep. He creaked open the door and stood in the doorway starring at her. Diamond noticed the shadow over her and opened her eyes.

"Bam Bam she said wiping her eyes"

"Well get a look at you. So ripe and innocent we would make so much off you" Juice said walking into the room. Diamond tensed up looking around for Bam
"Bam Bam Mika she cried out"

"Shhhh I aint going hurt you its cool relax. I like your night gown he said pulling her cover completely off exposing her bare legs. Nephew told me about that little tight pussy you been giving him. You mind if I peek for myself? He leaned in closer. Diamond grabbed the lamp next to the bed and smashed it over Juices head

"You little bitch he yelled"

She climbed over him and ran into the room where Bam slept

"Bam Bam she yelled but the room was empty she noticed the gun lying on the bed. Looked back and noticed Juice getting up running her way. She picked up the gun watching as Juice walk thru the door.

"I was just playing lil one, damn come here" Juice said still walking towards her

Loud shots echoed off the hollow walls. Diamond shot 4 times with her eyes closed

Mika screamed running up the steps while Bam ran out the bathroom and up the steps to the bedroom. Mika entered first "what's going on" she panicked

"Mika! Diamond cried running to her"
"What happened?" she asked Bam ran in and grabbed Diamond looking all over her body.

"Are u okay did he fucking touch you, he yelled. 2 shots hit Juice one in the chest and one in the head he laid bleeding on the floor

I'm sorry I'm sorry Diamond cried

Bam's heart slowly broke watching the fear and panic in her. "Baby girl listen to me you don't have to be sorry. No man should ever be trying to put their hands on you without your permission or you hurt them! Look at me is you hurt?"

"No, I'm not hurt I'm okay" she said wiping her eyes

Mika stood in shock looking at the dead body lying on the ground

"Meek look at me, take Diamond downstairs get her dressed and take her to eat or something while I clean up this mess. Mika couldn't take her eyes off the body. Mika listen to me he grabbed her face. Do what I told you get her dressed and leave this never happened I'll handle it"

Mika grabbed diamond and did as Bam told her.

Bam picked up the phone 330 543-2866

"Yo what's up what's the deal son long time no hear from" male voice answered

"Shit you know how I do, I don't really need your expertise no more I've been trying to stay straight if you know what I mean but yet again I got some garbage that need to be taken out" Bam replied

"Say no more my man, name the place and time and we there" Daeon said

"Right now my place"

"On the way" (OUT) they both said before hanging up. Bam paste back and forth trying to figure out how he was going to tell Druzy that Juice wasn't making it to the meeting. Bam picks up his phone:

Knock knock knock came from the front door Bam hung up his phone and proceeded to answer. Four men stood at the door dressed in all black with gloves on

What's the move? Daeon asked

"This way, he guided back to the room. I need to keep this on a hush until I figure out what the fuck I'm going to tell Druzy about this shit. I need this completely erased gone as if it never happened though" he said opening the door exposing Juice body on the floor.

"Bet he responded entering the room. Daeon looked back at Bam and smirked. Man, I don't even want to know what the fuck happened here I'm sure this rat deserved every bit of that shit! Nice aim though my man he joked flipping the body onto the throw rug

"I got to make a call. Take what you need to pack this shit up and take the back I'll see you in a second with pay full disclosure."

"Aright" they responded Bam left the room to find his cell phone so he can call Druzy.

"Look at the time and I hate to waste it" Druzy answered

"Listen man shit got fucked up!"

"I'm listening" Druzy responded

"Man, Juice came to the crib to pick me up to link with you but was acting weird as hell has was fucked up bugging going crazy, I think he was smoking that K2 shit"

"Get to the point nigga" Druzy said blowing his weed smoke

"He tried to reach in my pockets and pull my own gun on me! I had no choice but to shoot his ass man. I was aiming for his knee or something not deadly just to get his mind right, but it happened so fast I wasn't paying attention. I had to call GB to come clean this shit up if you know what I mean".

Both men sat quietly for what seemed like forever "Nigga first off that's too much phone time meet me on Jackson and Kirkpatrick at 11:30 clean that shit up leave no trace we'll talk then Druzy responded then hung up

Fuck! Bam yelled he grabbed his keys and left the house.

Text Convo: Babe I'm going be out for a minute, how is she?

Mika: She seems ok like it never happened we are eating ice cream right now

Bam: For real

Mika: That's how I feel, I tried to talk to her, but she said she's fine forgotten about it you'll protect her

Bam: Alright well keep her out get her nails and shit movies whatever keep her mind off it I'll call you to meet me back at the house later to talk to her before I take her back to Elliott

Mika: Ok Babe be careful please

Bam: Always……….

Bam pulled up to Kirkpatrick but no one was there. A black Audi pulled up behind him flashing his lights signaling Bam to get out.

"What's up man, Bam said getting in Druzy's back seat

"You tell me nigga one of my soldiers is dead! We got 15 girls held up"

"Look man I know"

"Don't fucking cut me off nigga, Druzy yelled our buyer been on standby he thinks I'm bull shitting that's bad for business! Now what happened?"

"Druzy I told you he starts bugging out tried to pull my gun I got him before he got me. I didn't mean to kill him, but I wasn't looking I just shot.

"I see, Druzy responded well this shit is on you… I need all them bitches drugged up and ready to go in 2 hours and none of them bet not look beat up on! Tell those niggaz to quit fucking them too having them all raw and shit. The connect is waiting at the Hilton on 30 he's expecting 10 girls for release and the other 5 take back after 5 hours so make sure your man's is on point! Bring back number 9, 3,8,7,2.

"I'm on it, he said sending a text with instructions

"Don't fuck this up make sure you count the money, 350k for the 10 girls and 30k for the 4. Meet me at dawn at the Denny's on McKnight"

"Got you, in a minute, Bam said exiting the car

Druzy watched as Bam pulled off. A black Infinity pulled up next to him and rolled down the window.

"So, what's the move, a male yelled out?"

"Something don't make sense to me figure out what the fuck is going on, Druzy said"

"Oh, I got eyes on his creep ass I'll have something for u in a minute: Beast responded

"Bet" they both said and went their separate ways

Bam pulled up to the tire warehouse on 62nd street. The warehouse was known for having the cheapest used tires in Youngstown. On the other half of the warehouse was where they kept the girls, drugs, guns and whatever was needed. They kept it completely closed off to the public and made sure it was sound proof. There were 2 warehouses one on the Eastside and one uptown. Over the years they manage to make over 3 million in the business completely invisible to anyone who wasn't affiliated. They had plug on the girls through the Cartel his name was

Hugo. He manages to ship at least 15 girls a month depending on the clientele. A lot of the guys just like to play with the girls and give them back but as of lately there has been big time purchasers and that's where the big money was at. The only rule was they didn't take any girls under 15 and for the most part they were runaways from the other side of the world, so they weren't too worried about no one looking for them. All in all, it was a smooth set up.

"Yo Bam yelled making his presence known

"What up, the guys responded

"Yo what the fuck you niggaz been doing we got an important drop in 2 hours why the fuck aint shit together, you seen my text"

"Relax Nigga they in the back it's handled, Cush responded" Bam proceeded to walk to the back

"Hold up, Rez jumped up we got a small problem"

"What?" Bam asked

"So apparently the Mexican/ Spanish cartel nigga didn't catch the memo cause we got 3 girls that aint supposed to be on the roster and they suppose to be moving out tonight Boss orders"

"What you mean, aint supposed to be here,"

"Follow me; Rez said walking to the back. The 2 entered the room that was filled with 15 half naked woman

"Yo shut the fuck up and sit the fuck down" Rez yelled

The woman sat down in fear and quiet down. Rez guided Bam back to where the girls were sitting crying in a corner.

"Uh yea so this is Ms. 13 Ms. 13 and Ms. 12, Rez pointed looking nervous" Bam stood just looking at the little girls, instantly brought flash backs of Diamond face.

"What the fuck is this? This aint going work get them the fuck out of here, he said grabbing them up, the girls screamed.

"No can do, you wasn't answering your jack so I ran it pass boss man he said they go tonight! Aint shit we can do now"

"I'll call him; Bam yelled walking out the room to call Druzy….

"Yo"

"Druz what the fuck is this you got 3 babies in here! That wasn't the plan"

"It's the plan now, there on the count. Don't worry about it the 3 of them on the 10 list so they won't be back minor slip up, but they'll be out of our hands so handle the business nigga.

"Man, them is little girls"

"Nigga handle the deal, or will this be a problem"

"It's done man no problem, Bam said hanging up

Bam walked back in the room with the worst feeling in the pit of his stomach. Just looking at the scared little girls made him hate himself because he knew things were out of his control.

"Alight nigga the Van is in the back the 5 can go in the truck the other 10 get all there shit together the drop is on West Shore"

"Got you, alright bitches let's go, Rez yelled

Bam walked over to the 3 girls "Hey I'm B, what's your name? The 3 girls clinched onto each other and cried. It's cool I'm a good guy, what's your name"

"Ms. 13 wiped her eyes I'm Nola this is Cyn... Bam eyes widened, and this is Déjà"

Bam just looked at Cyn but couldn't help but see the other Cynthia. Bam reached out for Cynthia she screamed causing him to snap out of his daze

"Nigga what is you doing Rez yelled'

"Just get the girls in the fucking truck! Bam yelled, listen ladies your about to go to meet my uncle he's really nice and he's going to take good care of you ok he's nice, but you can't cry he gets really upset when you cry be quiet ok"

"Yes, I understand Nola said"

"Oh, so you're the strong one out the bunch huh, Bam asked"

"I have little sisters I'm the oldest, she whimpered"

"Ok Nola is it"

"Yes"

"Make sure you take good care of them ok, it might not be great but it's not that bad once you get used to it ok"

"Used to what" she asked curiously

"Ok time to go Bam said follow the girls ok"

"Ok, she cried grabbing all the other girls to get up and follow. The girls all held hands as they followed the other girls to the Van.

"Man, if u want to fuck one of the lil bitches I can turn an eye Nigga" Rez jokingly said

Bam punched him in his stomach "Watch your fucking mouth and do your fucking job" Bam said Rez held his stomach in pain

"Aright man damn!" He yelled

The van and the truck driver headed towards the West Shore for the drop. Rez rode in the van while Bam followed in the truck. The look on them girls face wouldn't leave Bam's head: his phone rings

"What's up baby?"

"Hey babe, Elliot been calling he said he tried calling you, but you didn't answer it's getting late she has school tomorrow what u want me to do?

"Put her on the phone"

"Hello, Diamond said in the most innocent voice

"Hey baby girl, are you ok did u have fun with auntie Meek"

"Yes"

"Are u ok about earlier u can tell me"

"Yes, he was a bad man Bam Bam u said bad people need punished"

"Yes, I did say that, and u did good I'm proud of you, but you know you can't tell nobody right this is our secret"

"Yes, I know because I'll go to jail "diamond said

"No ill protect you nobody taking you anywhere, but people won't understand ok, so pinky promise our secret k"

"Pinky promise" she happily yelled

"That's my girl, well I'm still working late so Auntie going take you to get your stuff then drop you off to Elliott I'll be there in the morning for school ok"

"Ok Bam, have a good work" she said he smiled

"Thank you baby girl bye bye"

The 3-vehicle pulled up to the Hilton hotel at 9 o'clock sharp to meet the buyer. Bam had so many different things on his mind he didn't notice Beast tailing him the entire time. A car flashed its light inside the parking lot signaling Bam which direction to go. He waved the other cars to stay put while he drove in. Bam got in the back seat of the parked Denali:

"Well we meet again my fine young fellow"

"What's good Mr. Jackson how you" Bam asked

"I'm hungry and horny ha-ha, he laughed out loud, but I know you don't really care about that, Jackson responded pulling out a brief case. Here's what u want to count it, he placed the brief case on his lap

Bam opened the brief case and counted the money every penny was there! Bam texted Druzy (It's a go)

"Nice doing business with your Sir"

"Always a pleasure Bam, now can I get a whiff of that sweet candy" Jackson responded

"Wait here Ill wave the Van in"

"You see that Black bus at the end of the lot tell your guys to park next to that and the girls can get in there"

"Alright, Bam said opening door… he paused Uh Mr. Jackson"

"What's up man there a problem?"

"No it's just we had a minor slip up, there's 3 girls under 15 and they scared shitless just hoping you can take it easy on them you know.

"Listen here young fella; these bitches are in this world for one reason and one reason only! Baby pussy, grandma pussy, woman pussy, it's all the same thing and that's how I treat it. Get your heart out of this because you can't save these bitches and trust me it's going get a hell of a lot worse than better. So, to answer your question fuck no! Now take your money, deliver my bitches so I can get the fuck out of sight."

Bam got out the car and waved the van to pull up. The girls single filed got out the van and boarded the black bus, Nola made eye contact with Bam, but he looked away. She saw the disappointment in his eyes as she tried to fight back tears.

"I'll be strong" she yelled to him

Bam acted as if he didn't hear her as he watched the girls get on the bus. Nola got a window seat not taking her eyes off him. The 2 locked eyes until the bus was out of his sight.

Mika and Diamond got to Bam's house "Okay go gather all your stuff so I can take you home ok"

"Ok she said running upstairs"

When she reached the top of the steps she paused for a second then slowly pushed the door open. Everything was gone including the rug he fell on. No blood no evidence everything looked normal. She went into the back room grabbed her clothes book bag and doll.

"You ok you ready" Mika yelled

"Yes" she responded running out the room. Before exiting down the steps she noticed the gun still lying on Bam's bed.

"Diamond, come on boo its late" Mika yelled again

Diamond grabbed the gun and put it in her book bag and ran down the steps.

"All ready' she said

"Yeah let's go" Diamond said smiling….

Chapter 6 (You are strong for yourself even stronger for others but not all the time) One must take off the armor and be weak to gain strength
{HEARTRENDING}

"Cedes, Cedes, Diamond Yelled running up the steps"

"What damn what the fuck u screaming about"

"Something is wrong with G-Pap,"

The 2 ran downstairs and noticed Elliot lying on the floor groaning holding his chest.

"Oh my god Daddy, are u ok, Mercedes cried"

Diamond ran and got the phone and called the cops

"9-1-1 WHATS YOUR EMERGENCY" My Papp needs help

Mercedes grabbed the phone from Diamond hello my daddy is having a heart attack I think, were at 2498 Singapore Rd. please hurry"

"Ok ma'am an ambulance is on its way"

"What the hell did u do, Mercedes yelled slapping Diamond in the face" Diamond cried nothing "Daddy she yelled be strong help is coming"

The ambulance pulled up to the house Elliot was barely breathing, they rushed in. Checking his pulse, it was very faint, so they gave him an oxygen tube and rushed him to the hospital. He had to go alone because Mercedes was the only adult there with Diamond and her twins.

"Can we go to the hospital please Cedes, Diamond cried"

"You are not my responsibility so don't ask me shit" she replied'

Diamond ran into her room and cried. She loved her aunt despite how she treated her all she wanted to do was make sure Elliot was going to be ok. Bam bought her a cell phone to use in case of emergencies so she called him.

"Hello" he answered

"Bam Bam, she whimpered"

"What's wrong baby girl you are crying?"

"G Pap is hurt he was lying on the floor grabbing his chest and he went to the hospital I asked Cede to take me, but she said I'm not her responsibility and hit me in the face" she cried

"What! She hit u! I'm on my way" Bam replied hanging up

"Yo I got some shit to do I'm out" Bam said to Rez

"Nigga we got 5 keys that need broke down in the next 2 hours how the fuck I'm pose to do this shit b myself"

"Family business man, where Teh and Daeon at"

"You know Druzy want them watching the girls and out this part of the business from now on cause of that shit on the North side"

"Fuck! I'll be back a.s.a.p. this important"

"What's could be more important this money Nigga! It's that little girl huh"

"What the fuck you say!" Bam replied

"Chill Nigga I'm your man 100 grand. If u got a little secret daughter u clearly don't want nobody to know about that's cool with me that's your business especially with the shit we into I wouldn't want nobody to know either.

"You don't know what the fuck you're talking about!"

"Listen I already overheard that nigga Beast telling Druzy about her."

"What the fuck Beast doing around?"

"Doing what he does best Slime balling trying get his next come up off who and whatever. He seems to have it out for you though. I kept it to myself cause if need be Ill handle that issue for you feel me. So, is he going be an issue?"

"Not yet but he might end up being one feel me! Between me and you that's his daughter! Don't ask questions long story but I owe her mom, so I took lil shorty under my wing."

"Nigga huh, Man I don't even want to know. So, he knows that's his daughter?"

"Nah he knows he got one but don't know who she is, and I want to keep it that way feel me"

"No doubt we'll keep your eyes open he up to something. Go head though I'll hold it down make it quick kid" Rez said extending his hand for a handshake

"Bet in a minute" Bam said embracing his gesture

Bam arrived at Elliot's residence to pick up Diamond Mercedes answered the door

"Who is it" she yelled peeping out the door she noticed it was Bam. When she opened the door, he punched her in her face.

"Bitch, don't ever put your fucking hands on her. I will fucking kill you he said standing over her"

"I didn't touch her she cried"

Diamond came running down the steps and noticed Bam standing over Mercedes

"Damn girl you got be careful he said helping Mercedes up off the floor. Hey baby girl you ready? Go get your coat so we can go see your Pap to make sure he's ok"

Diamond grabbed her coat off the couch and left with Bam

"Is u ok? Let me see your face" Bam asked

"I'm ok I don't know why she's always so mean to me. The twins don't like me what's wrong with me Bam Bam?

"Nothing is wrong with you Diamond your aunty is a miserable mean person and you're amazing. Miserable people don't appreciate good people like u and honestly you shouldn't want to be nice to her either because it won't matter, she will always be unhappy and she's teaching her kids to be the same that's why they daddy aint around either"

"But Bam my daddy aint around either"

"That's different though"

"How's it different? Who is my daddy? Do you know?"

"We can talk about this later ok we're here let's go check on Elliot" he replied pulling up to St. Elizabeth

Bam and Diamond walked into the hospital and up to the receptionist desk.

"Hello, I'm here to check on a patient that just came in about an hour ago"

"Ok and what's his name"

"Elliot Waters"

The receptionist checked the computer for Elliot's information.

"Ok I'm going to ask you to take a seat and the doctor will be out to speak with you in a second are u family"

"Yes and alright thank you" Bam said

He walked Diamond over to the waiting area. Mercedes walked in with the twins and spotted Bam and Diamond.

"Anything" she asked in a panic Bam looked at her with a look of disgust

"NO" he responded

The doctor walked into the waiting area,

"Family of Elliot Waters, he said"

"Yes, that's me, Mercedes replied"

"Uh can I speak with you in private away from the children" he asked Bam Mercedes got up and followed the doctor away from the children

"How are you related to the patient?"

"I'm his daughter"

"He's my uncle, bam replied looking at Mercedes waiting for her to deny it"

"Okay well unfortunately Mr. Waters didn't make it! He had a severe atherosclerosis which caused his coronary arteries to become blocked. It's been going on quite some time now un-noticed or maybe there weren't any symptoms or signs but unfortunately there was a plaque rupture and clotting in his heart muscle that we couldn't resolve in time which lead to his death I'm so sorry"

"No not my daddy, Mercedes cried"

Diamond noticed her aunt crying and the look on Bam's face told her it wasn't good news, she began to cry to herself. Mercedes ran over grabbed the twins and ran out the hospital. Bam looked at Diamond with such sadness in his eyes realizing she had no one now.

"Baby girl I got some bad news, he said sitting down"

"I know Bam G-pap is dead, she cried hugging him"

"He's in a much happy place now, G-pap was in a lot of pain, but he hid it and smiled for your pretty face every day! Look at me he said wiping her eyes sometimes people die bad people die in pain but the good people like Elliot die happy so you shouldn't be sad ok Diamond"

"Ok but now I have no one left to love me, I'll have to be an orphan" she cried

"I love you and you know Bam will always take care of you ok wipe your eyes"

"You promise?" she asked wiping her yes

"I promise"

Ring ring ring,

"Hello he answered"

"You have been doing this disappearing act more than usual lately! What's up with that we got work in the loop" Druzy said

"I'm on my way back now I had a little family emergency really quick Rez is handling business though"

"Rez aint in fucking charge nigga, and if u can't play your position you won't be either" Druzy said hanging up

"Fuck! Listen baby girl I got to take you to your Auntie for just a little while then I'll be back to get you Bam got to handle some business okay"

"Please don't take me back to her she hates me please" she cried hugging him

"Ok ok you can stay with me. Come on let's go"

The two left the hospital Bam drove around downtown trying to get in touch with Mika to take Diamond for a while but she didn't answer the phone. It's already been 2 hours he's been gone so he decided to drive down to the warehouse with Diamond.

"Listen I need to run in here really quick and finish up some grown-up stuff. Can you be Bam's big girl and wait here for me? You can play your tablet I won't be long ok"

"But it's dark and creepy out here"

"I know but I'm right here wont nothing happen to you I promise. Look you see that light, he said pointing I'm going right in that room and I'll be peeking out every 2 seconds okay"

"Okay" she said

He handed her the tablet and some skittles before closing the door. Diamond watched as Bam walked away disappearing into the doorway. She turned Catfish on and ate her candy. Druzy was gone when Bam got back and Rez managed to break down more than half of the package.

"Yo" Bam said

"Listen man I didn't says shit to Druzy he just popped up looking for you and I didn't want to tell him where you were."

"It's all good let's just finish up pass me the scale"

"Did u handle your B.I" Rez asked sliding the scale

"Yea man shits just all over the place but ill handle it just stick to the mission."

Beast pulled up to the back of Bam's car when he noticed a small screen lit from the back seat. He got out his car and walked past looking in the car only to see little Diamond laughing hysterically at a show she was watching. She didn't even see him walk up on the car. Interesting he said to himself walking into the warehouse.

"Well since when does such fresh meat get personal rides boss man" Beast yelled out getting their attention

Bam ran to the door to check on Diamond who was still safely sitting in his back seat.

"Oh, so he has a trigger I see he laughed who's that your little girlfriend! Little young don't you think!" Beast joked

"I'll bust your fucking head" Bam yelled walking towards Beast

"WhoaWhoaWhoa chill yall damn business" Rez jumped up to intervene

"Yeah business" Beast replied with a smug look on his face walking away from Bam… Well Druzy sent me here to collect, this don't look like 9 hundred and thirty bricks am I missing something?"

Bam went over to a box on the table and pulled out the remaining bagged bricked

"Nah you aint missing shit" Bam said

Bam and Rez packaged up the bricks and sealed them in bulk with plastic wrap and stuffed 5 ceramic owls with the product packaged them in 5 card board moving boxes and taped them shut. Each grabbed the boxes and walked them out to Beast's car. Bam kept his eye on Beast as he kept his eyes on Diamond.

"Keep your fucking eyes to yourself nigga" he said

Beast kept walking laughing to himself. Diamond noticed Bam walking past the car and opened the door

"Hi Bam Bam" she yelled smiling and waving

"Hi baby girl close the door I'll be there in a second"

"Ok, she said closing the door"

"How cute I see why you're so emotional" Beast said loading the boxes in the truck

"Mind your fucking business nigga" Bam relied"

"Man will you niggaz relax, Beast you got what u need tell Druzy to hit us with the next move be out my nigga" Rez said defusing the situation again

"Fuck this nigga I'm out" Bam said walking to his car Rez I'll hit you tomorrow"

"No doubt "Rez replied

"Yo B she's gorgeous my man keep her close. It's obvious she means a lot would hate to see anything happen to her? Beast said sarcastically

"Was that a threat Nigga" Bam said walking towards Beast. Bam punched Beast in the face causing him to fall to the ground and kicked him in his face with his boot. Fuck you bitch ass nigga" bam yelled

"Bam Bam Diamond yelled

Rez rushed over and broke the fight up between the 2 "Just go bro, Rez yelled pushing Bam to his car

Bam got in his car and drove off

"Well at least we know where his heart at hope we never have to cut it out huh" Beast said to Rez getting in his car and driving off

Bam drove in silence he knew it would be a matter of time before he must get rid of Beast for good

"Bam is you ok' Diamond said in a low voice

"Yea baby girl I'm fine just a little argument that's all"

"Is he a bad man? I seen him with Auntie Cedes when I was little"

"Oh yea" he said remembering that Mercedes twins were also Beast kids yes he is a bad man if u ever see him without me you run and scream ok"

"Okay"

"But you don't have to worry about that Bam's always here, lay down get so rest were going home k

"Okay, she said laying in the backseat"

1 week later

October 28th the day of Elliot's funeral... Diamond had been staying with Bam since the day of his death trying to figure out exactly what to do with her. He didn't have kids of his own and knew that he couldn't take her on full time. She hasn't been to school and he been leaving her with different people while he ran around handling business, it wasn't the life he wanted for her. He decided to take Diamond to the funeral for last goodbyes and possibly run into a family member that can help him with her or even take her under their wing.

"Diamond you ready it starts at 11"

"Yes, I'm coming"

Diamonds came down the steps in a pretty dress Bam bought her.

"Don't lie how u like what I did with your hair seriously" Bam joked

"Uh it's ok but why is this sticking up," they both laughed

"Aright here let me try this he brushed and tucked it into a bun see I'm learning"

"Now u know this is going to be a sad view of your G-pap, but you have to be positive remember he's happier now and his soul is smiling probably watching you so you really just looking at his body ok"

"Ok"

"Cool let's go"

Bam and Diamond pulled up to J&D Mason Memorial Funeral Home just as the doors were closing to begin. The two-ran making it just in time. It was a full house but they managed to find a few seats in the back. Diamond looked around confused as to whom all the people were. She could see Mercedes and the twins in the front row and all the way in the front she seen Elliot's body lying in a casket. She grabbed Bam's arm tight and put her head down.

"Good morning and welcome everyone! I see a lot of sad faces a lot of hurting hearts, but I want you to know we are not here to mourn the death of our fellow love one Elliot but to celebrate his life. The Lord Jesus has taken away the sting of death through his resurrection. Believers know that for all who are in union with Jesus, their bodies will be united to Christ after death and they anticipate the hope of the resurrection. The sting is gone. The last enemy is defeated. Death has no victory over the believer. All of this is true in a spiritual sense—death has lost its sting, victory over death has been won. Death no longer holds us captive, but as a pastor for nearly a decade, I have observed that death and the trials and sorrow surrounding it have stings that catch many families by surprise. We never know when we will be called out of this life. Middle-aged men die; children die; old people die. Unless Jesus returns, we will all die. There will be mourning; the sting of death will bring pain. But trust me in this—if you are in Christ, the mourning will be only here on earth; you will be face-to-face with your precious Savior, Jesus Christ. If u believe in that can I get an Amen?

"Amen"

Elliott was a serious and disciplined man, but he could never resist the opportunity to have a laugh with friends and loved ones, given half the chance. He saw a lot during his lifetime: a world ravaged by war, (he was himself served in the armed forces in Vietnam), all understandably influencing his views on the post-war world in which he himself grew up and, later, raised his own family. Let alone the social and cultural revolution exploding around him with the onset of the 1960s. So, you see he then seen some things folks and honestly, he got to live his best life Amen

"Amen"

Alright we got a short poem from Ms. Mercedes Water daughter of Elliot Mercedes can you come up here please?

" Good morning everyone! This is called Rest Angel written by me…. Don't think of him as gone his journey has just begun. Life holds so many aspects here on earth this was just one. Just think of him as resting from sorrows and from tears. In a place of warmth and comfort where there are no days or years. To the living he is gone and unfortunately will never return. To the selfish you were cheated but its god will you must learn. Although I can't see I know your presence is near, I will hold you close in memory until I drop my very last tear. My feelings are bittersweet I must say I'm really torn it's hard to celebrate when all I want to do is mourned. As sad as I feel I can't help but smile you're probably looking down on this crazy family smiling back at us right now. We won't say goodbye but so long for now, this is tough for us so make sure you send a sign every once in awhile. I love you dad" Mercedes cried returning to her seat

"That's was beautiful Mercedes Amen! At this time, we are going to close this ceremony with a gospel song sung by Sister Roberts. We want everyone row by row to say your last goodbyes to Brother Elliot we also will have a small gathering downstairs food will be provided thank you."

Sister Roberts began singing a piece by Yolanda Adams as everyone took their time weeping their last goodbyes to Elliot. Bam wasn't familiar with any of the faces at the funeral so he just stayed in the back with Diamond.

"You want to go up Diamond"

"Yes, can you come with me" she asked

"Sure, come on"

Bam skipped the rows and walked Diamond up the Elliot's casket.

"Wow you look just like you mama!" an unknown woman said catching both their attention are you her father" she asked

"Nah friend of the family and you are?" he asked

"I'm Ethel Ann her Uncle Henrys ex wife lord bless his soul and her mother. Cynthia was a good girl so sad her father didn't see it especially when Diamonds a spitting image. Look at me running my mouth how is she holding up?

"Uh well were here she's ok as she is going be for now, Bam answered feeling a bit out of place

"Well here's my number I know this family can be a bit much and with Elliot being gone who's to say what will happen to this poor child. Listen u call me anytime ok baby"

Diamond didn't take her eyes off Elliot's body.

"Diamond I'm a go talk to your aunt Cedes real quick put Ms. Ethel Ann's number in your phone and save it I'll be right back you ok" he asked

"Yes"

"Yo Mercedes peep game real quick"

Mercedes sucked her teeth as she stood up to walk his way "Look I don't need your shit it's my daddy's funeral" she snapped

"Bitch pipe down ill smack the fuck out of you and I'm not here for that. What are we going do about your niece she don't have nobody now" Bam plead?

"There aint no what are WE going to do. You wanted her so bad right well she's all yours. I'm taking my kids and moving to Pittsburgh with a friend so figure it out" she said

"You would just do that to your blood! What she ever do to you? You one fucked up bitch you and your bastard kids. You should have had that nigga Beast bust on your face instead now you bringing up two fucked individuals that are going be just as fucked up, broke and miserable as you. Get the fuck out my face"

Mercedes stormed away with tears in her eyes. Diamond stood watching all the people at the funeral and no one looked familiar. Were they family friends what, no one offered an open arm or condolence she felt so alone and Bam noticed that look on her face?

"Diamond lets go aint nothing here for you. You said your goodbye's right"

"Yes, but I'm so sad" she cried

"Listen he said kneeling down to her height you have to realize even as a youngin everything happens for a reason bad and good. This just happens to be bad, but I got you. You never have to worry about Cedes again want to know why? We are leaving here and going to buy you a new bed and toys and clothes for your new room at my house"

Diamonds face lit up like a Christmas tree

"Really"

"Yup so fix your face! Come on let's get out of here"

Chapter 7 (Close your eyes to see that something even if you that something seems distort) Beautiful nightmares so everlasting while sweet dreams are cut forever short {**CAUSTIC**}

4 Months later

"Diamond is you ready?"
"Do I have to go back to school?"

"Yes, you do, education is very important. Now that were settled and you're getting back to normal with everything you've been through the past few months we need to get back to life "Bam said

"Ok I'll go just got to grab my bag" she responded

Diamond had missed 2 1/2 months of school last report period and enjoyed her summer trying to get things back in order. Mercedes did as she said she packed her and her kids up and left. Bam knew he had to do all the proper paperwork to get custody of Diamond and he did. She had no family, so it wasn't a hard process. She went through a spell of nightmares/terrors for the first month some about Elliot's death and shooting Juice. Her initial reaction to everything as it happened Bam assumed, she was fine but when everything hit her at once and she realized she was not ok. He took some time to help get her back to the normal sweet child she was. Now after 4 months he feels like she's ready. A meeting with the principal was scheduled to go over some things and try to get her back on track to graduate with her starting class .Bam and Diamond got to the school just in time for the 8 o'clock meeting with

Principal Puzio. While walking to the office Diamond noticed Jayson walking in the hallway, his eyes lit up with happiness while Diamonds stomach cringes at the sight of him. Jayson disappeared into the class while they disappeared into the office.

"Hello, you must be Mr. Nichols" Mr. Puzio said

"Hi yes I am, Bam said standing to shake his hand

"Right this way, Puzio guided them into the office; ok let's take a seat Diamond it's a pleasure to have you back"

Diamond smiled

"Ok so I see a lot has changed since the last time she was here. It looks like now you have full custody of Diamond Mr. Nichols. I just want to sincerely say I'm sorry for your loss Elliot was a great man I knew him from church"

"Thank you, Bam replied I really just want everything to be a smooth transition. Just get her back in school back to normal being around kids being a child you know"

"Absolutely that's the plan! I spoke to her teacher she gathered up a packet of all the missing work, but she can come back a start alongside everyone else"

"Ok that's cool"

"Alright Diamond, if you're ready I can walk you down to Mr. Clowski's class

"Yes, I'm ready, bye Bam Bam"

"See you later be good Mika will be picking you up."

Mr. Puzio walked Diamond to her class

"Knock knock look who I found, he said entering the class"

"Hello and welcome back, everyone take time and welcome Diamond back" Mr. Clowski said

"Welcome back Diamond" the class said

"Ok Diamond we were just finishing up our packets. You can go and take a seat on with everyone and I'll get your things. I manage to speak with Ms. Greiner to fill me in a little on who you are and what is needed to make this year great for you"
Diamond went and found a seat when she noticed Jayson starring a hole through her. She looked through the packet she was given trying to avoid eye contact when she felt someone behind her.

"I missed you. Where did you go?"

"Don't talk to me, she responded"

"Why you are being mean, I love you"

"Listen; if you say one more word to me I'll shoot you dead like your bitch ass uncle!" Diamond said

Jayson looked at her surprised, he couldn't believe the words she said to him he leaned in "Stupid bitch" he whispered before running away Diamond smiled

A group of girls called Diamond over to sit with them for the class project

"Hi, I'm Taffy this is Mila and Alanah we wanted to be friends earlier in the year, but you disappeared"

"Oh, yea my G-pap died"

"Oh my god was he murdered? Mila asked"

"No, he had a heart attack" Diamond snapped

"Sorry, we seen Jayson bothering you don't pay him no mind his Uncle got murdered so he's been acting all crazy" Taffy said

"I'm not worried" she responded knowing it was because of her

"Ok class I seen everyone grouped up that's great I'll give everyone 30 minutes to create a group design of your ideal summer day"

The girls put their heads together and began to draw up there perfect summer day with her new friends

Rez and Bam were asked to meet up at Mills Mall to discuss the new business package. Druzy informed them both that one of their biggest clients Hector Hernandez had a special request but neither of them had any idea what it was all they knew is it was a lot of money. Bam pulled up

Rez was already standing outside his car blowing on his vape.

"What's good my guy "Bam said

"Aint nothing up but this weight your heard" Rez replied

"You know what the move is yet?"

"Nah but there go Druzy right there, he pointed

Druzy pulled up with Beast in the passenger seat. There was still a lot of animosity between the 2 for several reasons but they didn't let that interfere with business for now they tried to stay out of each other's way unless it was necessary. Bam and Beast caught eye contact as Druzy stepped out his car. Beast was using his hand as a gun gesture as he pointed at Bam. Bam smirked and looked away.

"Fellas prompt like I like it. So, let's get down to business he said handing them 2 yellow folders. This is Daphne she's 13 she goes to Marion-Sterling School in Cleveland so you niggaz got to travel a lil bit. Now the reason why this one is a little special is she aint no run away! She's a little innocent girl from a good family so no drugs and you niggaz don't touch her I'm sure Hector wants personal use but payout out of this world. So, the snatch is going to have to be thought out and smart. I picked today because every Tuesday her afterschool program lets them go to some Bumba Mumba playhouse shit."

"Wait how the fuck we suppose to snatch this girl from a playhouse there's mad eyes cameras and shit and 13 we at this again" Bam said

"Yall my dream team make this happen no questions or do you need Beast's assistance?"

"Fuck no, Rez said"

"Well we good then, get moving my niggaz clocks ticking, meet me at the spot when the mission complete" Druzy said getting back in car

"Damn man it's always some wild shit with this nigga, this is an actual kidnapping now"

"Chill nigga we do this! We can take this buggy it got woofers in the back. Duct tape the bitch toss her in the trunk put the sounds on and ride out what's the deal" Rez said

"Us getting caught" Bam replied

"Nigga you can chill after this pay out its Hector we are talking about! He singled out this bitch so he willing to pay something crazy. So, let's just do it man we out" Rez said jumping in his Mercury.

Bam followed behind jumping in the passenger seat. The 2 hit the 1-80 heading towards Cleveland it was 11am still early enough for them to do there outside research and find the right time and place to make the move. They arrived at the playhouse about 1:20 pm after discussing the plan they decided that Bam would go in and tour the facility while Rez went to the school to check it out.

Ding Ding

"Hello how can I help you?"
"Hello, my name is Quinton Jones me and my family are new to the area. I have 2 sons ages 12 and 11 and they'll be attending Marion-Sterling. My fiancé was told by the principal that a lot of the parents use this place for after school care, so I thought I'd come and take a tour just to see what it was like" Bam explained

"Okay yes definitely I would be more than happy to assist you. Where are my manners, I am Debbie Wheeler one of the mangers here at the facility? We have 4 workers on board usually most of the day. After 2pm the bigger kids start to arrive (which if you joined would be around your boys ages) and the younger ones are picked up, so we usually only need 2 peers on board that's what we call the workers. Follow me we can look around.

Ok this here is our toddler room I know you don't need this but it's part of the tour so I'm giving the whole kit and caboodle she laughed. This is our main office where most staff are, well at least someone to get any information needed. Our doors are always locked, and you must sign in to take your child out. We have a playground in the back, but it's accessed through our rear door which is right here. As u can see it's gated in decent size for the kids to play around if they want. To the right is our little study hall/computer lab most of the bigger kids have access to the internet unless the parent prefers something different. These are the bathrooms and here is our wall of all our dreamers that's what we call all our participants here and there places in age order. Don't you just love kids?"

"Love them, Bam responded going through the photos on the walls

Bam received a text from Rez {Leaving the school now bus should be there in 2 minutes}

"Do you have any children that go here?"

"Unfortunately, I don't have any kids, but my brother's daughter Daphne comes to keep me company she also attends Marion and honestly, I love all my dreamers like my own, so it works out. Did u have any questions?"

"Uh yea can I take a look at some paperwork maybe get some prices?"

"Sure, come right this way into the office" The two walked into her office and she grabbed him the paperwork to go over. Will you excuse me the late bus arrived I just need to get everybody in and settled just one sec. she said leaving the office

Bam could see the school bus pulling up. He pulled out his cell – {playground back window blue it go up then out got me eyes open}

Bam sat in the office pretending to look over the paperwork while he secretly watched as the kids got off the bus. Daphne was the third person off the bus. She had ear buds in her ears as she walked into the building without removing them and he didn't take his eyes off her. Bam's phone rung it was Diamond! Daphne walked into the office

"Oh, oops didn't see you scared me sorry just grabbing bathroom the pass excuse me," She said reaching over him"

Diamond called back again he ignored her watching Daphne walk into the bathroom while Debbie was still trying to get the rest of the kids off the bus. Bam followed behind. He waited until he heard the water running to open the door, he pulled out his gun.

"Shhhh you scream and I will shoot you and your precious Auntie Deb. Open the window" Bam said Scared Daphne did as he said Rez was standing outside the window.

"Damn nigga this one landed on our lap that was quick as hell" Rez said jokingly Daphne cried

"Nigga quit playing and grab her before somebody come in" Bam loudly whispered in anger

Rez helped grab Daphne out the window groping on her butt and legs. "You pretty as hell, Rez said pushing her into the backseat. Bam walked back out to the office without being noticed and sat back down. "I apologize these kids are all hyped up probably cause it's Friday" she joked

"Oh, it's no problem at all, I'm actually going to take this paperwork with me and get back to you. My fiancé called and need me to pick up the kids so I got to run but I will definitely be in touch this lace looks perfect" Bam said

"Well that's good to hear, well here our card call us any time droning business hours, and someone here can help ok. It was nice meeting you" she stood to up extending her hand

"You too have a good day" He said exiting the building. He continued to walk off the premises and down the unknown street before calling Rez. Rez pulled up next to him sweating with a small scratch on his lip.

"What happen?" Bam asked

"Nothing that little bitch feisty though" he responded

"Pop the truck" Bam demanded he walked back to the trunk looking around to make sure no one seen him. Opening to the trunk Daphne lay bleeding from the nose with her pants half down. He slammed the trunk and got in the car

"Nigga what the fuck you do! He said untouched"

"She aright we can wipe her little nose bleed and she will be cool" Rez plead

"You raped her; she was probably a virgin you don't think he is going catch on to that shit stupid motherfucker"

"Man, you worry too much we good family" Rez said getting on the turnpike

"Fuck, this aint going end good" Bam said

"Relax I got it covered, he said blasting the music to out sound Daphne's screams.

Diamond hung up after her now 7th call to Bam's phone with no answer. Mika never showed up to get her from school she didn't have her phone number, and everyone was pretty much gone for the day. She didn't know the exact miles it was to Bam's house but had an idea of how to get there on foot if needed so she decided to walk hoping maybe he just fell asleep and didn't hear his phone. Diamond walked through the school yard and exited onto Southern Blvd. She remembered driving this way numerous times when he dropped her off and picked her up. She remembered at least 5 stop lights before turning onto Elis Drive where the house was. She zipped her coat kept her head down and walked the Blvd trying not to get anyone's attention just eager to get home. She crossed the street when she got to the basketball Court. Looking up to cross the street she noticed 3 groups of guys playing basketball.

"Diamond, is that you? A voice yelled from the basketball Court. Hey bitch you hear me calling you. Diamond realized it was Jayson and began to walk faster.

"Hey Diamond! Bitch answer me, remember what you said about my uncle" he yelled following behind her. She managed to get 3 lights up the Blvd before finally stopping

"What the fuck do you want; she yelled yeah I remember what I said"

Jayson slapped her across her face! She quickly grabbed her cheek and began to cry

"I'll fucking kill you, he yelled grabbing the back of her neck and throwing her to the ground.

Diamond scraped her knee causing her stockings to rip with blood pouring down her knee.

"Ouch Ouch, she cried you said you loved me."

"I don't love you no more stupid dummy fuck you"

But I love you! She said drying her eyes I want you to kiss me and touch me again?"

Jason looked confused but she had a serious look on her face

"Huh you want me to kiss you" he replied

"Yes, can you? I missed you while I was gone"

Jason leaned in to kiss her but Diamond blocked him.

"Let's walk over here where no one can see" Diamond said

The two walked to the back of the Eagle Ridge apartments. There was a small playground with a swing, slide, see-saw bench and water fountain.

"Can I kiss you now?" he asked

"Sure, but let's get on the see-saw for a little bit my knee hurts" she said limping

"Sorry about that, I just get so mad"

"Mad huh where you think that comes from your uncle?"

"Don't bring him up! He's the only dad I knew now he's gone, and no one knows why" he put his head down sadly

"Can I ask you a question? Then we can kiss and whatever" she asked taking her book bag off and sitting it on her lap

"Ok" he responded smiling

"Why were you so mean to me? Why did you touch my private parts? Did no one ever teach you that was wrong?

"That's what people do when you like somebody.

Everybody do it not just me"

"That's not true no one has ever done that to me! I was scared and I didn't like it at all.

"Well that's what my uncle taught me, well before he died"

Diamond reached in her book bag and pulled out the gun she stole off Bam's bed. Jason's eyes got big as he raised his hands in the air.

"Whoa wait what u doing"

Diamond began to cry again

"Your uncle was wrong you don't do that to people! He was a bad person and that's why he's dead"

"Okay okay Diamond please put the gun down"

"Say it"

"Say what I'm scared please don't" he cried

"You and your piece of shit uncle are bad people"

"Me and my uncle are bad people please don't shoot me"

"Your Uncle Juice was shot with this same gun because he tried to hurt me. I was going to tell my uncle Bam to kill you, but I had his gun this whole time to do it myself" she said cocking the gun.

The bullets shot out the gun in slow motion as it pierced Jayson's chest. He fell from back from the see-saw causing Diamond to fall backwards to the ground dropping the gun. Jayson laid gasping for air just like his uncle did. Diamond grabbed the gun and her book bag and ran back in the direction of the school in a panic. She tried calling Bam's phone again this time he answered:

"Diamond did Mika pick you up"

"Bam I shot him I shot him" she cried still running trying to catch her breath

"What! Where's Mika what's going on?"

"She didn't come! I was calling you! You left me here alone!"

"Baby girl, where are you?"

"I'm almost back at the school, I have nowhere to go"

"IM ON MY WAY STAY THERE" Bam yelled in a panic How far are we from the YO

"Like a good 15" Rez responded but no detours nigga that lil bitch loud as hell you hear her. Can't risk it already told Druz to meet us up the spot"

"You got to handle this shit solo, drop me at Miller Elementary I'll deal with Druzy later"

"Damn nigga you keep flaking when I need you, I'm not trying meet Hector by myself he fucking crazy and the girl got a mark on her face I need backup in case she try to lie or some shit." Rez said

"Listen I don't give a fuck about him Druzy or you nigga drop me the fuck off" Bam yelled

"Damn it's like that? Fuck me I'm your mans! We bout to get paid! All over that little BITCH maybe Beast need that info to get her out your hair"

Bam pulled out his gun "what the fuck you say Nigga"

"Chill man I wouldn't do that I just don't understand why she's so important to you"

"It's not your business to understand" he yelled with the gun still pointed

"Put that shit away nigga I'm on your side! We here man"

Bam hopped out the car and ran into the school yard

"I'm out man I'll try to work something out with this shit" Rez yelled pulling off

"DIAMOND DIAMOND" Bam yelled as he searched around the school playground. He spotted her sitting underneath the slide crying with her knees clinched to her chest. He raced over to her

"Come here are you ok what happen whose blood is this? He asked in a panic checking her for wounds.

"Jayson's I shot him he touched my private like his uncle tried to" she cried

"What you mean his uncle! Oh shit Juice! Realizing she kept the gun FUCK! He yelled Baby girl listen to me where was this at? Did anybody see you?"

"In the back of Eagle Ridge I don't know I just ran I was so scared" she cried

"Come on he said pulling her arm show me where you was at"

Bam and Diamond walked out the school yard and exited onto Southern Blvd noticing several cops' lights 3 blocks down the road

"Shit! Come on let's go back to the house"

Rez pulled up to LaTora a private club that Hector owned and was advised to pull to the rear private lot. Entering through the gate into the private lot he noticed Beast and Druzy counting 4 Louis Vuitton totes full of money

"Now we talking", he yelled out the window parking his car. Rez got out the car smiling and rubbing his hands "Yes yes happy birthday to me he said over the muffled screams coming from the trunk

"You a man short aint you?" Druzy said

"Yeah, I know but as you can see business is handled, he said pointing at the trunk

"Where he a..."

""Fellas welcome, Hector said interrupting it sounds like our little plan worked out just perfect. Hello my sweet girl he said knocking on the trunk. Give me the key is she tied up or what don't need any surprises"?

"Well now we aint have time it was a rush job, so we just shoved her in there after taping her mouth up and rode out" he said throwing the keys

"No worries my friend, this little shot should help her relax!"

Hector opened the trunk Daphne eyes widened while she kicked and screamed Hector put the needle in her neck causing her to pass out.

"My sweet precious I will make you love me he whispered rubbing her face. What is this? He asked pointing to her eye"

"There was a misunderstanding but it's just a small little scratch she'll be cool"

"The fuck you mean misunderstanding! This is unacceptable she looks beaten! Druzy your guys treat her like a Puta De Mierda! He yelled angrily

"She's good damn, it was a little scratch Druzy bumpy ride you know how shit be" Rez said

"Rez you know Hector is one of our special clients! Your job and mine is to make him happy. So, Hector how can we make this right?" Hector pulled down her pants and noticed the swelling in between her legs.

"He touched her! I want his dick cut off maybe he'll learn to keep it to himself" Hector said waving a few of his guards to come out

"What the fuck that's not going down like that" Rez yelled backing away from security...

Security grabbed him

"Hector man please okay it was an accident she was wilding out"

"You had precise instructions" Hector yelled

"It was Bam! All I know I got out went in the store came back out she was bleeding from her nose with her pants down. I can't say what happened. I asked he told me to put her in the trunk and drive, so I did" he plead

"Wait a minute! Where is number 2 Druzy" Hector asked

"He had some other business with a few girls to handle back at the warehouse" Rez responded

"I wasn't aware he would've touched her. My exact words were Untouched and honestly that don't seem like shit he would do. Rez is you sure that's how shit went down" Druzy asked

"Man on everything that's exactly how shit went down"

"Call him and tell him to come to me!" Hector said

"I'll do you something better Beast you go get him and bring him back here" Druzy instructed

"Now we talking, that's music to my ears, Beast said grinning. Rez you lay low and keep your mouth shut I got it from here Nigga"

Chapter 8 (Money aint the root of all evil attention is) Ones clock tick while another's still tock using it wisely makes all the difference but then again maybe not {PETRIFY}

"REZ CALL ME THE FUCK BACK NIGGA I BEEN HITTIN YOU FOR 2 DAYS SHITS FUCKED UP I HAD TO DUCK OFF BUT I NEED THAT GUAP" Bam screamed into his voicemail

A sketch of Diamonds face flashed across the 6ocklock news {Have you seen this girl} if so, please contact the Youngstown police department immediately!

The sketch was of a young girl who appeared to be a shade darker with a narrower face than Diamond but whoever the witness was managed to get her Unicorn book bag and curly pig tales. Bam took Diamond and went and stayed at the Spring Gardens hotel by the Pittsburgh airport for a few days so he can figure out his next move. He had been calling Rez but didn't get an answer in the past 2 days, so something had to have gone wrong at the drop with Hector an Druzy.

{Ring Ring} it was the 15th call from Mika

"What Up" Bam answered

"What up what up nigga where the fuck you been! I have been calling you nonstop worried sick! I went past your house it's all fucked up! Is something wrong! Are you ok? What's going on babe? I see the news too; please tell me that's not Diamond! I recognized the book bag I got her it was a dead fucking giveaway. What did you get her into Bam?"

"Chill the fuck out, he whispered. I can't do this over the phone, but I need your help! Shit got fucked up and I don't know what's going on! I need you to find Rez for me on some seen without being seen type shit if u catching what I'm throwing. Shit is mad shaky right now, so I need you to switch rides with Sissy and ride up the way. See if you can get in contact with Rez one way or another if you can either way hit my 814 number at 6 from a different phone and I'll tell you where we at to come through"

"Cool are you 2 safe? Is she cool?" Mika asked

"Here Diamond" Bam said handing her he phone

"Hello" she said

"Hi baby girl are you okay" Mika asked

"Yes, I'm fine. I did a bad thing again"

"What I tell you. It's not bad if it's done to bad people. Was he bad?"

"Yes, really bad like his uncle" Diamond replied

"Then you did good ok baby girl"

Diamond looked at Bam who had his face planted in his hands

"Ok, Is Bam Bam mad?" she whispered

"No just a little stressed he wants the best for you for all of us. But we are going be ok. I'm going to go for now baby girl, but I'll see you later"

"Ok, Diamond said handing Bam back the phone

"Yo" he answered

"Babe she needs you now, she's just a baby for real so make sure you comfort her! I'll hit your line at 6 on the dot love you ok be safe"

"Love you too, out" He hung up

Diamond sat on the edge of the second bed of the hotel facing the wall with her head down. Juice and Jayson's face flashed before her eyes along with the loud gun shots. Tears filled her eyes while she sat still trying to keep it together, She wasn't sorry for what she done but for the trouble she may get in or other people in for her actions

"Diamond come here" Diamond got up and walked over to Bam wiping her eyes

"It's ok to cry. It's just mean you have a big heart and emotions. Listen I'm not a good guy at all I killed too! A lot way more than you and you still think I'm awesome aint that right" he smiled

"Yes"

"I'm new to all this too! I never had a kid let alone a daughter, so I don't know how to be that good role model dad type. I know how to survive. So am I mad at you no some niggaz got to die period! Don't matter the age especially when it comes down to you or them! You always chose yourself hear me.

"Yes"

"Now I'm sure you see me over here bugging but I'm a little stressed. I got a little situation on my side with my business and someone seen your face baby girl, so they got a sketch of you on the news."

"Am I going to go to jail?" she asked worried

"Hell, no over my dead body! What I tell you Bam will always protect you no matter what. Mika just got to turn your pretty curly hair into something straight and different just to make sure you're off the radar"

"Straight will be pretty too" she said with a smile

"Of course it will! Want to know a secret when you got a pretty face you can wear anything and still be gorgeous remember that. And I noticed there's a swimming pool so when Mika get here you can go get your hair all wet before she make you look all fancy deal" he said jokingly

"Deal" they laughed

Mika decided to pop up on Sissy at her spot hoping she would run into Rez. Sissy was her father's step sister who lived on the North side of Youngstown. She had an undercover gambling hub everybody knew as "The Basement" everybody that was anybody ran through that spot for one thing or another. She sold everything from single cigarettes to birth control pills to A.R fifteen. Her son was leader of the Eastside Laws, so she was off limits and well taken care of hence not to be fucked with.

"What's up Auntie" Mika said walking in

"What's up doll face, what are you doing around these parts stranger?"

"Shit just chilling, I was actually looking for my dudes' friend! He been missing in action and I know when niggaz go missing you can find them losing all they money in the basement and shit" she laughed

"Girl and you aint never lied I see first-hand how these niggaz be tripping but go ahead you can walk through there's wall to wall heads down there so I'm sure he in the crowd. Who is it?

"Rez black ass"

"Rez yea I seen him yesterday but don't think I seen him today but go head down there and see I don't know child I'm high" Sissy replied opening basement door

Mika did her walk through and as usual the basement was packed! To the right was full blown money loaded crap games and to the left was live strippers making money. The Bryn Mawr boys were in the building but no Rez. She spotted Raymond & D. Nails Druzy's young dumb trying to get ahead fuck boys who would do just about anything to prove they worthy to the old heads. More than likely they probably the ones who kicked in Bam's door and trashed his crib she thought. She usually wouldn't have even spoken to none of them, but she needed the info.

"What's up has anybody seen Rez?"

"I mean who asking" D-Nails replied

"What! Don't act like you don't know who I am! Yall seen me around the way plenty of times"

"Yeah, might have but you are walking around all serious asking questions like the feds so what's up"

"What's up is, me and Rez got some shit to talk about not really your business so again have you seen him or not"

"Talk to Marlon he was just with him." Raymond said pointing to the guy in the wheel chair in the corner.

Mika proceeded to walk over in his direction

"Where Bam been" Raymond hollered out

"I thought you niggaz didn't know me" she responded sticking up her middle finger and walking away

"I bet that bitch know exactly where he is. You know Druzy looking for him too"

"Yea that bitch knows" Raymond responded

"Yo let's cut! We going follow her and let her lead us straight to him, Druzy will break us off something lovely if we do" D-Nails said smiling

"Let's be out"

The 2 slipped out the side entrance while Mika attempted to get answers out of Marlon

"Yo, I need to talk to Rez I was told you knew where I could find him"

"Yeah I might but who you" Marlon asked

"I'm pregnant with his baby; I need to talk to him"

"No baby girl, that can't be true you Bam's bitch.

Mika, look in astonishment, exactly that's why I need to talk to Rez

Shorty Bam is my man so you can keep it real he need to get at his man I know Rez got him all caught up. Last I checked he was down on 20th digging the tunnel if you know what I mean. Tell Bam the wolves are out hope he washing the blood off cause they sniffing."

"Oh, he got shit under control" she said walking away

Ray and D-Nail watched her walk away right before making a call to Beast.

"What up Beast this Ray, didn't you tell me niggaz was looking for Bam?"

"Yea is he up the way" Beast asked

"No he still out of sight but his bitch up here looking for Rez, kind of fishy huh"

"Cat fishy! It's cool I'm going have him show face one way or another. Keep an eye open if anything shake let me know matter of fact you little niggaz follow her"

"I'm already on it! We sent her to Marlon I'm sure he told her Rez was up 20th that's the direction we are going right now"

"Alright call me if anything changes, I'm on my way there now. Make sure she don't spot you" Beast said before hanging up

Mika rode up 20th where she seen Rez standing outside of Circle K talking to some woman.

"Rez what the fuck" Mika said hoping out of her car

"Mika what's up, he responded looking nervous"

'Bam been trying to reach you for the past 3 day's nigga why you duck off"

"Duck off I'm right here aint nobody ducked off"

"You know what I mean, what the fuck is going on?" she yelled

Rez noticed D-Nails car sitting on the corner as Beast pulled up slowly behind them.

"Shit got fucked up bad, Tell B I'll be in touch but stay out the way till I figure some shit out"

"Listen I'm supposed to call him at 6 why don't u meet me and talk to him or at least call his 814 number he's bugging out."

"Mika I'm going to get at him, but you got to get the fuck out of her niggaz know of you too. I'm going to handle shit swear but get up out of here like Asap

Mika looked around and noticed Raymond starring at her. She looked back at Rez who was giving her a look of concern. She started laughing as if he said something funny "Alright Rez let me go I'll tell her she been tripping for no reason and you aint up to shit with her pregnant emotional ass" she yelled loud enough for other people to hear

"Exactly tell her ass to lay low and keep her head down the baby will be here soon I'm handling business out here securing the bag feel me, but I'll call her at like 6" he responded

"Okay she said getting back in her car"

"Aye watch out to the cops is fucking with everybody and they are being sneaky following everybody thinking they got something feel me" he winked making sure she was aware of what he was really insinuating

"I'll talk to you she said pulling off"

Beast called Raymond and D-Nails

"I think she spotted your whip but follow her anyway she won't see me coming if she worried about you"

"Alright" D-nails responded pulling off behind her

Mika drove through the Southside of Youngstown with Raymond and D-nails 3 cars behind her. It was 5:55 so she pulled over to call Bam and make him aware of what was going on.

{814-398-2394} "What's up babe" he answered

"Ok this is going go fast because I got some of Druzy's fuck boys following me"

"D-Nails?" he said

"And Ray but I got a plan I'm about to spin these niggaz. Oh, and I talk to Rez, but we can talk about that later be expecting a call though. Where am I going?"

"PGH Airport Spring Hills 303"

"Ok baby! I'll be late but I'll be there ok love you" she hung up racing back to her car as they watched. Mika drove around for about 20 minutes until she reached her apartment; she grabbed her things and went inside. D-Nails called Beast to inform him of their location. Mika gathered her things and called her friend Tasha. She advised her to meet her at Mills mall by Macys in 30 minutes then she called an Uber to pick her up. Mika left her apartment with a stuffed overnight bag and stood outside next to her car. Ray and D-Nails were confused as to what she was doing until a blue Taurus pulled up and she got in. The 2 followed her and let beast know they were on the move.

"Describe the driver" Beast asked

"Black old woman I don't know could be her raise or some shit"

"Hmm could be stay on her I'm going chill back at her place maybe Bam might show his face"

"Ok"

The 2 continued to follow the car that soon pulled up to the Macys at Mills mall. Mika got out and went in catching site of Ray's car, just as she planned. D-Nails got out following her in the store. Mika grabbed a few shirts a pair of pants and disappeared into the dressing room. She called Tasha

"Hey Girl you out there"

"Yup right by the bus stop"

"Cool here I come"

"Cool"

Mika left the clothes in the dressing room; she peaked out the door and noticed D-Nails scrolling through his phone facing the opposite direction. She slowly crept through the clothes ducking low so she wouldn't be seen and quickly exited out the store. She cut through the food court where she spotted Tasha sitting waiting for her. "Go girl go" she yelled hopping in the car and reclining her seat all the way back. Tasha drove off

"What is going on girl" she asked

"You know niggaz be thirsty had to spin his ass left him on stuck, he probably still waiting for me to come out the dressing room" she said laughing

"Girl you crazy where u going"

"Oh, take me back to my car at the crib please"

"Okay are you going somewhere? I see you got your overnight hoe bag" she said laughing

"Long story but yeah little quick run I'll be back in 2 days" Mika said

"Girl you always up to no good" Tasha said pulling up to Mika's apartment. Alright chick be safe don't do nothing I wouldn't do"

"Bitch what wouldn't you do" Mika joked getting out the car. She threw her things in the back seat of her car jumped in and texted Bam (OMW) not realizing that Beast was parked at the end of her street watching her. Bam responded ok and she pulled off. Mika merged onto I-76 headed towards Pittsburgh not realizing Beast was right behind her. His phone rang

"Man, I don't know how but we lost her"

"Of course, you dumb niggaz lost her" Beast yelled

"She was right there though" D-nails plead

"I got shit under control get back to business will be in touch" he said hanging up

The 2 drove for an hour and half Beast made sure to stay as far behind as possible without losing her or being noticed before reaching the Spring Hill Suites. Mika was so excited to see Diamond and Bam she didn't even think to check her rearview mirror. She pulled in to the parking garage and called Bam to meet her outside. Beast parked close enough to see everything without being spotted. Diamond and Bam came outside to greet Mika

"Mika" Diamond yelled running into her arms

"Hi, love she said embracing her

"What's up Babe everything cool, no extra eyes" Bam asked looking around

"I shook them niggaz fucking amateurs" she gloated

"Of course, baby I taught you well let's go in" he said

"Yeah I wasn't sure how long we was going be"

"Mika, they have a swimming pool" Diamond said excited

"Really I can't wait to go" Mika said walking into the building

"Well they closed at 8 so yall can go tomorrow" Bam said

"Awww man I was so excited to go,"

"We can still do some fun girls' stuff though k"

"Ok" she replied entering their room

"Diamond I'm going talk to Mika right outside the door ok watch your show I'll be right back" Bam said

The 2 entered the hall

"You talk to Rez"

"Yeah, he was acting so weird but said he fucked up, but he was going make it right and said he would call. He started talking in code because bitch ass Ray and Nail was following me. I ditched them in the mall and had Tasha grab me to take me back to my car and came straight here"

"And no one followed you right"

"Baby no one I was extra careful. Are the cops looking for Diamond?"

"They only got a sketch! They reaching for questioning she should be cool. There's mad kids out here that could past for that sketch but to be safe just change her hair"

"Ok I'm so happy you're ok. Is there beef with you and Druzy now?"

"Babe I don't know shit. Nobody answering me I'm lost for real. Our last job went smooth so I don't know what's going on"

"Well I'm here we'll figure this out together" she said hugging him

The 2 went back into the room as Diamond was closing the curtains to get ready for bed. Beast spotted her through the window. "Jackpot" he said to himself calling Druzy

"Talk to me" Druzy answered

"Well well guess who I'm looking at right now" Beast said

"Who's that?"

"Bam and his little family playing house down Pittsburgh at the airport"

"The Airport, Is he going somewhere?"

"Looks like he just camping out at the Spring Hill Suites. I followed his bitch and of course she led me straight to him. He hiding for a reason guess Rez story checked out"

"Good to hear! I'm sitting here with Hector now. We got good news sir" Druzy said we found Bam and his lady

"Oh he got a lady too? Hector asked, we go there and take them all, I will make his lady one of my new girls" he laughed

"You heard him we coming to take everybody. You sit tight keep your eye on them. We are making a grand opening like fireworks on his bitch ass."

"Ha-ha that's what I like to hear. They are getting comfy for the night so take your time I got this" Beast said

"My man see you in a minute" Druzy said hanging up the phone

"I'm sorry I have to do this to one of your good men you told me so many good things, but I had strict rules about the job, and he ignored them and let his dick do his thinking and touched my precious butterfly. I can't let that type of disrespect go" Hector expressed

"I understand some soldiers rise others fall so be it"

CHAPTER 9 (Learn to escape your mind) One's thoughts can drive you crazy. Ones actions can drive you wild. Your strengths will surprise you when forced to change your lifestyle {**CONTEMPTUOUS**}

Next Day

Rez pulled up to the warehouse. Druzy's car was parked in the lot along with Hectors H3 and 2 other random cars. He walked in confused as to why Hector was there.

"Whoa nigga, can't be sneaking up on me" Druzy said loading his bag with 2 40 caliber pistols and halo bullets

"My bad what's going on? What's up Hector" Rez said Hector gave him a head nod and lit his cigar

"Beast got the drop on Bam so we bout to run down on him"

"Run down what you mean you going kill the nigga?" Rez asked

"Not quite!" Hector said

"Meaning"

"Well Beast said he got a young girl with him nice and tight, his woman aint that bad either. And as you know we are in the Right and Tight Bitch business! So, we about to recruit 2 new ones and if Bam don't follow suit them POW! Druzy explained

"Come on Druzy his girl, Mika you joking right? What the fuck is up with that? We supposed to be family we don't go against shit like that. And the little shorty like 9-10 or some shit like his little sister come on Druz that can't go down like that Bam won't allow that.

"Nigga, do I look like I'm propositioning options! He knew the rules he didn't follow there's consequence to every action. Hector makes me matter fact us good money got to keep him satisfied" Hector looked at him with a slight grin of satisfaction on his face

"Where did he find him at" Rez asked

"He down Pittsburgh at the hotel by the airport Beast sitting on him"

"No doubt, here go that 20k I did all my rounds so I'll see you tomorrow taking my moms' to the casino down West Virginia" Rez said

"You sure you don't want in on this action partner" Druzy asked

"No you know moms be tripping off this gambling shit!"

"Ha ha yea I feel that"

Rez walked out the warehouse and got in his car; Druzy Hector and his 2 bodyguards walked out behind him and got in a black on black suburban. Rez watched as they pulled up. He picked up his phone 8 1 4 5 5 5 4 6 3…… He hung up

"Fuuuuuuckkkkkk" Rez screamed feeling guilty about what was about to happen

Mika took Diamond to the store to buy the 2 swimming suits after the complimentary breakfast at the hotel. Bam stayed back in the room making calls trying to figure out what was going on in the streets.

"Hello" Daeon answered

"Nigga I need facts! Your ear been to the streets" Bam asked

"Who this"

"B"

"Oh, what's good Nigga you sound all jittery and shit couldn't catch your voice, what's good?"

"Nigga I'm bugging the fuck out, this nigga Rez aint answering Druzy M.I.A I hear motherfuckers following my girl what's really good"

"Well you know me and squad had to go clean up some messy ass shit at Sissy spot. Some young nigga got mad about a crap game and shot 2 niggaz! But I ran into your mans"

"Who Rez"

"Hell yea all paranoid and shit. You know I'm the FAM so he starts spilling shit. Apparently your man's put his foot in his mouth with the big wig some Italian nigga or some shit"

"Ok Hector" Bam replied

"Right, so I'm guessing you niggaz had a job and the product came back tampered with. Apparently it was his daughter! Papi was pissed trying like cut off Rez dick or some shit"

"What! His Daughter! Bam repeated

"Yea or some shit. So peep the fuck shit though to save his own ass he said it was all you. So now niggaz is on a hunt. Ya girl came up the way and them stupid niggaz tried following her but I guess you taught her well because she left them niggaz on stuck" Daeon said

"That's why that bitch ass nigga aint answering his phone. Dog eat dog man that's supposed to be my man"

"I mean he said he had a plan to fix it, but I don't see how. The Italians play no games especially about family so unless he plans on clipping dude it looks bad for you"

Mika and Diamond walked back in to the room

"Bet appreciate you I'll hit you in a minute if anything changes hit my jack"

"No doubt Fam" Daeon said hanging up

"Bam Bam look! Diamond said flashing her bathing suit aint it pretty

"So pretty" he said

"Babe you ok?" Mika asked

"Yea I'm straight just figuring shit out" Bam said

"Ok cool, well us girls are about to get our suits on and head to the pool are you coming"

"Yea you 2 go head I'll be down in a minute"

"Ok"

Mika went in the bathroom and her and Diamond got changed and headed down to the swimming pool. There were 2 other children in the pool when they got there about the age of 8-10 years old, but they weren't accompanied by any adults. Diamond grabbed an inner tube and jumped in while Mika sat on the edge of the pool.

"Hey u want to play with us the 2 girls asked" "Yeah, Diamond answered looking at Mika for approval Mika nodded

The 3 girls splashed around in the pool having the time of their lives. Mika had her head down scrolling through her phone. Beast sat outside the glass window at the lobby bar to the right of the pool watching waiting for the call from Druzy.

"Would you like another drink sir" the bartender asked Beast phone lit up with a text message that read HERE at your truck!

"No thank you, bill it to my room John Smith 207" Beast said

"Alright Sir, have a good day"

Beast excited the bar and proceeded right of the pool as Bam was walking towards the pool from the left completely missing each other. Beast spotted Druzy and hopped in the back seat.

"What it do" he said smiling

"Good work my guy you are good on my book" Hector said to Beast

"Thanks, the girls are in the pool right now. Bam still in his room"

"How many people in the pool area all together?" Druzy asked

"Altogether 4 two little white girls about 10 Bam's girl and the little girl"

"Who is the little girl? Bam aint got no kids."
"I don't know but the one day he had her in the car I said 2 words to the little bitch and he snapped the fuck out so it's somebody important to him"

"Good! He fucked with my girl I fuck with his girls" Hector said

"Alright well we can grab them now Bam's in the room. Put them in the car then put the gun to Bam and make him follow behind us"

"I got Bam's room; you grab the girls, Hector you just relax! Shit if you want you can take them other 2 bitches too" Druzy joked

Bam entered the pool area.

"Uh oh baby girl look at you. You think you can swim huh" he said Diamond laughed
"Is that your dad?" the girls asked

"No that's Bam, Hey Bam watch this Diamond said getting out the pool. Diamond ran as fast as she could and jumped into the pool making a big splash. Mika and Bam cheered her on. Beast slowly crept from the rear end of the pool when he noticed Bam sitting next to Mika.

"Shit" he whispered he pulled out his phone and text Druzy's {Bam's in the pool area we need a distraction}

"So, what's up I seen it all in your face" Mika asked

"I spoke with Daeon this nigga told me Rez than put my name into some bullshit with Hector about our last drop. I don't know how deep but niggaz is looking for me."

"What could he have said though was anything missing"

"No basically he put me in his place on some fucked up shit he did and he supposed to be my mans"

"Oh, that's what he meant"
"What"

"When I ran into him, he said I fucked up but I'm going make it right"

"Aint no making it right! If I got bad blood with Hector aint nothing changing that especially about this. So, I got that on top of Diamond killing Juices nephew. Aint no real heat but I don't know because I'm ducked off out here trying to keep her away from the bullshit"

"Baby and I know she's thankful for…." The 2 were interrupted by Bam's phone ringing.

"Yo" Bam answered

"Man, shit got fucked up" Rez replied Bam's eyes got big

"Rez what the fuck is going on, he hollered Mika I'm going to the room real quick" Bam said walking out.

Beast texted Druzy {coming your way} as he watched and waited for Bam to disappear out of sight.

"Chill I got everything handled" Rez plead from the other end of the phone

"Nigga I spoke to Daeon he said you told Hector I hit the bitch and stuck my dick in her when I kept telling you not to fucking touch her now niggaz got money on me"

"No, it wasn't like that, but that nigga crazy he tried to put the knife to me! I just needed to buy some time but you my man's I'm going handle it"

"How nigga! You aint shit no clout no weight. You run behind me you might need to be watching out too shit you might be setting me u p now" Bam yelled opening his room door

Druzy caught the door with his foot before it closed all the way

"Now you know me better than that my G just give me some time" Rez plead

"What's up Nigga hang up that phone" Druzy said from behind him. Bam slowly took the phone from his ear keeping his hands up

"Listen Druzy! It's not what you think you…."

"Shut the fuck up" he said picking up his phone

"Yeah" Beast answered

"I got him make that move" Druzy instructed

"Bet" Beast said hanging up

Bam could see his gun next to his bed but couldn't risk getting shot trying to grab it.

"Get your keys let's take a ride nigga" Bam did as instructed. Him and Druzy head down the stairs to his car.

Mika was still scrolling her phone looking up every few minutes to check on Diamond not realizing Beast was now sitting behind her in a fold out lawn chair. Diamond got out the pool to jump in again when she noticed Beast.

"Hey! You're the bad man Bam Bam was fighting" Diamond said pointing to Beast. Mika turned around to see Beast holding his gun on his lap.

"Don't be stupid bitch, he whispered to Mika smiling. It was a small disagreement but we're ok now. He invited me up here to kick it aint that right" he responded

"Yea baby girl it's ok, keep swimming" Mika said holding back tears

"Actually, it's time to go we got pizza and chips waiting so grab your things let's all go" Beast said grabbing her towel.

Mika collected her things and helped Diamond put her bottoms and flip flops back on. Diamond could see the gun on Beast waist as she began to walk towards the exit door.

"Where's Bam Bam"

"He's waiting for us, come this way" Beast said

"But I don't have my stuff" Diamond said

"We got everything let's go now" he said becoming aggravated

"Come on were fine Mika said"

Beast walked behind the 2 until they got outside. The black Suburban sat on the right of Bam's car where he sat in the driver seat waiting. Diamond held Mika's hand until she spotted Bam.

"Bam Bam" she screamed running toward his car. Beast grabbed a fist full of her hair picking her up off the ground. "You aint going nowhere"

"Get the fuck off of her," Mika screamed and swung her arms hitting him. Bam tried to open his door but Druzy cocked his gun back pointing it at the temple of his head.

"You move and I'll blow your brains out"

Beast punched Mika in the face causing her to fall to the ground. The passenger side bodyguard picked her up and put her in the car. Diamond cried as Beast shoved her in the car with Mika.

"Drive Nigga" Druzy yelled to Bam as the truck followed

"Where the fuck am I driving to" Bam mumbled

"Cleveland we got 2 new girls to get rid of" Druzy whispered

"Come on Druzy I can explain everything you don't go to do this"

"Shut the fuck up talking is over Hector probably having fun with them right now" he said as they drove off

Bam looked through his rear view where he could see Diamond sitting in the middle of the row next to Hector crying.

"I'm going to take real good care of you" Hector said rubbing her head smiling

Chapter 10 (If a tree falls in the forest yet no one heard it did it fall) you're too young to know the truth too old to believe it left too prideful to accept it {**ANGRY**}

Mika woke up in a large room full of woman of all ages. She ran to the window the view to the street that was at least 6 stories down. The other girls in the room just stared at Mika as she shuffled around trying to find Diamond.

"Diamond she yelled but didn't see her anywhere Diamond"

"Shhhh be quiet they get mad when we yell" Nola said

"Who's they?" she asked

"Mika" Diamond yelled

"Diamond she yelled back following her voice

Diamond was in the room next to hers that was separated by a glass door.

"Baby girl are you ok" Mika whispered at the door

"No I'm scared, where's Bam? What's going on I can't get out" she cried

"Listen I don't know what's going on but be brave I'm right here ok I'm going to get us out of here" Mika said

"Who is that over there? Your sister" Nola asked

"Where are we" Mika yelled

"Stop yelling they won't answer we're in some building up really high. Me and my sisters been here awhile they shipped us from Youngstown. I overheard a few guys saying someone will be here to take us soon. The 2 big black guys come in here and take turns with all of us, so if she's over there by herself they have something special planned for her! Maybe all of them will have her" Mika slapped her in the face.

"She's a little girl" she yelled

"So are we until we do something about it" Nola said walking away

Mika sat down by the glass door, she could here Diamond crying. The door on Diamonds side opened. Mika could hear the same voice from the pool.

"Don't be scared come here sit down where it's more comfortable" Beast said walking towards her Diamond pushed back onto the glass door.

"Mika please" she cried

"You better not fucking touch her" she yelled through the door

Beast picked Diamond up off the floor; she kicked and screamed as he placed her on the couch.

"Shhhh I don't bite its cool relax! I just want to ask you a couple questions relax. Here have some water" He said handing her bottle water. Diamond looked at him suspiciously as she grabbed the water and wiped her eyes.

"See now aint that good, he whispered rubbing her head. Now first things first who are you? Are you Bam's daughter niece cousin what?" Diamond just looked at him and didn't say word. "Be nice to Beast I gave you water" he said smiling trying to put her at ease

"Where's Bam"

"He's in the next room he'll be in real soon. Now answer my question who are you"

Diamond looked him in his eyes smiled and said "Fuck you" as she kept drinking her water.

"Ha-ha fuck me huh" He repeated before slapping her across the face causing the water to fall to the floor.

Mika continued to bang on the door screaming for help. Diamonds nose began to bleed as she cried. Beast pushed her down on the couch and ripped her shorts off. She kicked as hard as she could but he laid all his weight on top of her. He tried to cover her mouth with his hand but she bit him.

"Get the fuck away from her" Mika screamed causing a bodyguard to come into the room.

"Quit screaming old bitch, he yelled grabbing her by her hair. Oh you're the new one! Do you a want to see what we do to the new girls" he whispered rubbing his hand across the crotch of her pants

Nola ran over and stabbed him with a pen in his neck while Cynthia her sister jumped on his back stabbing him with a rusty nail in his ear. He screamed swinging

Cynthia around trying to get her off his back. Mika fell to the floor trying to loosen the frontal of her wig where she kept her mouth razor. She noticed the big bodyguard lying over Cynthia's body chocking her .Mika ran up behind him placed the razor to his neck and cut right to left. He fell over holding his neck trying to stop the blood, but it kept running out. Mika put her knee over his face to mass the grunt noise until he went silent. The girls in the room just looked at her scared and confused. Mika grabbed his keys and proceeded to get to the room where Diamond was.

"There are too many people they will kill you" Nola muffled holding her ribs

"Well I got to do something" she said jiggling the keys trying to find the right one to unlock the door

Beast forced Diamond onto her back and ripped her swimming suit bottoms off. Diamond wasn't strong enough to get away. Beast spit in his hand to lubricate his penis and forced it inside of her. Diamond screamed in pain as he brutally took away her innocence. Visions of Jayson's face flashed before her eyes. Is this what she deserves? Is this what death feels like she thought? She suddenly went quiet as Beast pulled out and came on her ripped bottoms. He sat up and pushed her on the floor and threw and towel at her.

"Fuck me; wipe up that blood lil bitch! Guess you aint as grown as you thought. Wait until I tell Bam I popped his sister's cherry. He laughed you thought that was bad it's going to get a lot worse he said as he zipped his pants. He noticed the silhouette at the glass door trying to get it unlocked.

"Yo who that" he said

The movement stopped on the other side of the door.

"Maybe it's your brother coming to save you; Beast said pulling out his gun. He slowly walked over to the door slowly opening it. Peeked out the door but no one was there. He turned back to in the room. Give me my damn water ungrateful bitch" he said to Diamond while she laid on the floor crying. Mika ran up kicking him in his testicles from behind causing him to hit the floor then she kicked him in his face grabbing his gun. Déjà and Cynthia ran in behind her

"Oh no, she sighed looking at Diamond bleeding on the floor she rushed to her. Diamond I know you're hurt but you got to get up"

"Beast laughed; bitch you really think you getting out of here? I should've killed you first right along with your bitch ass boyfriend."

"You go find a way out of here; I'm going to kill him. Did you kill Bam? She said holding the gun to his face

Déjà and Cynthia helped Diamond up, they walked out of the room and Nola was waiting signaling them to be quiet. The hall was long but no one else was on the floor with them. None of the other girls dared to follow along fear of being killed so they closed the door behind them as they crept past the door. They were whispering amongst each other trying to figure out the smartest way to go when Diamond heard Bam voice from another room.

"Hey who's there" he yelled

"Bam" Diamond yelled as her eyes got bright. She limped over to the door and opened it. Bam sat tied up to a table in the middle of the floor. Diamond rushed to him as she cried

"Who did this to you" he panicked as his heart slowly broke

Diamond tried her hardest to UN tie the rope around his hands

"Wait a minute I know you! You're with these guys" Nola said

"You don't know what you're talking about, he said. Baby girl let me out before anyone comes" Diamond looked confused but didn't stop trying to get him loose

"Look at my face! You put me and my sisters on that bus in Youngstown! I spoke with you I told you my name"

"I didn't have a choice!" he yelled not completely free

Diamond looked at him puzzled as she freed his hands.

"Come one baby girl, he said picking her up wrapping her up with his shirt let's get you some help" He walked towards the door

"Nah nigga, Beast said hitting him in the face with the butt of his gun. The girls ran behind Bam while Mika cried with the gun to the temple of her head with her face and mouth pouring with blood.

"These little bitches of yours feisty but I handled lil mama she a woman now. Now I'm wondering if I should fuck your bitch before I kill her too"

"You one sick motherfucker, do you know what you just did Nigga! Do you know who this is?" Bam plead in disappointment

"Yea somebody important to you and that's all that matter check this out don't blink nigga" Beast said cocking back his gun

Boom! Mika's body fell to the floor… The girls screamed

"Shut the fuck up! Beast yelled. The bitch was too old anyway now the rest of you bitches get back in the fucking room NOW"

"Beast this is Cyn's daughter! Cynthia Waters this is your daughter nigga" he said in between his chokes

"Fuck you talking about my daughter"

"Beast you remember that night don't play fucking dumb" Bam said

"Oh, that night we both fucked her while she was unconscious or the night we went in her crib and you watched me slit her throat"

Bam rushed Beast into the hallway causing them both to trip over Mika's dead body...

"Run Run Nola said" grabbing Diamonds hand. Diamond didn't take her eyes off Bam as she ran away from the both rolling on the ground fighting for the gun. Barely able to walk Diamond ran with everything she had in her. The girls reached the fire escape door. After much effort Déjà managed to get it open.

"Come on, she yelled" Diamond took one last glance at Bam. He was standing over Beast's beaten body with the gun pointed at him.

Boom! She heard one gun shot. The girls kept running when they noticed the 2 vans pulling up on the side of the building.

"Shhhh, stay up against the wall and run to the left of the building when I say go OK"

The girls nodded following Nola

The fire escape door swung open

"Diamond, Bam yelled"

Diamond looked back

"Baby girl please dent runaway I'm sorry let me explain, he said walking towards her. Diamond kept running and managed to make it to the bottom of the fire escape.

"Diamond, come back please" he yelled running down the step after her

"Boom Boom Boom, shots fired hitting Bam's back causing him to fall down the steps.

"Bam Bam, she cried out running to him"

Druzy and 3 other body guards crept around the corner to see Bam lying in the middle of the fire escape

Cynthia grabbed her before she was seen "No! We must go or you will die"

Beast limped down the fire escape and shot 3 more times looking directly at Diamond as she watched him. He dropped the gun falling to the steps as the guards help carry him back into the building without speaking a word of the three escaping.

"What the fuck happen" Druzy said walking in

"Man, shit got fucked up, most of the girls still in their"

"Most I only see Bam's bitch laying here leaking, you killed more" Druzy asked

"No a few got away through that door I tried to catch them, but it was too late I only caught B going down the side, so I popped him. As you see the nigga got to my piece and shot me first" Beast explained

"It looked like he beat your ass! How did he even get loose or your gun nigga?"

"I don't know where was your mans that was supposed to be watching him. Them bitches got loose and fucked me up too"

"Fuck all that if they got away we need to relocate Asap" he said picking up the phone. "We need a bus we got to change locations NOW gather up the girls were out in 20. Beast clean yourself up we got business to handle" Druzy said walking out the room

The 4 girls ran for their lives and came upon a planet fitness gym.

"Listen walk in keep your head down and go into the closes bathroom ok" Nola said

The girls nodded doing as she said it was 1015 pm and only a few people were working out. Cynthia went first and the girls followed into the bathroom. The 3 girls went through each locker in search of whatever they can find. Diamond went to the shower turned it on sat down and let the water run over her body. She silently cried as the blood washed from between her legs. She was all alone again and the guy who is responsible for everything was her father. He took her innocence and the only person left that loved her was dead. What will she do now she thought?

"Hey, I found you some clothes and some underwear and towels" Déjà said sitting down on the floor outside the shower. I'm sorry this happen to you Diamond but we got to all be there for each other now. Me and my sisters are from Mexico and we can't get deported back to that terrible place. Our daddy sold us without thinking twice all 3 of us and kept my brothers. These 2 big men came and took us in the middle of the night while my daddy just watched." Déjà said

"Kind of like that man back at the building did u call him Bam? He was a nice guy when I spoke with him in

Youngstown before he sold us too. He was just as bad as everyone else" Nola interrupted

"Bam Bam was good to me" Diamond said

"But it came with a price he raped your mother, Cynthia said shutting off the shower. Look I know you're sad and I know you're hurt but we got to go so let's pull it together and get dressed. Were all hurting but I found a phone and have a plan but we have to go. Do you have anyone or anywhere we can go?"

"No! No one" she cried

"Ok its fine we got you you're going to be ok! Nola what about Auntie Tauti she might be surprised but maybe she'll help us"

"Oh, yea ok try 411 they may have something" Nola said

Cynthia dialed information and asked for a number to Tauti Lopez of Fredericksburg Va. They had 1 listing for a Tauti Lopez phone number 504-309-3432. She dialed her number and it rung and rung finally a Puerto Rican ascent answer

"Hello"

"Hello, can I speak to Tauti"

"This is Tauti who is this"

"This is Cynthia your niece. Me Déjà and Cynthia are in trouble"

"Wait wait, who? Marla's daughters how did you get this number? Where's your mother? Wait you girls are in the states?"

"Daddy gave us away to some bad people Tauti please help us" she cried

"Oh my Jesus on the cross! That sorry piece of shit! Calm down where are you now"

"We escaped a warehouse in Cleveland and ran far. We snuck into a planet fitness gym for clothes and I found this phone, but we can't stay here we have to leave soon.

"Ok is there anywhere you can stay and be safe until I get there? 6 hours tops!"

"We will figure out something were going to take this phone it doesn't have a charger so we will try to reserve the battery. We will wait to hear from you Tauti please come.

"I'm on my way stay safe" she said before hanging up

The girls continued to collect anything they could to take with them.

"Do you think your aunt would mind me being with you?"

"I told you we all are going to stick together trust me you'll be ok now" Déjà said

The girls snuck out the bathroom with a gym bag full of things.

"Hey Ms! Hey, get back here" one of the employees yelled

Cynthia grabbed Diamonds hand

"Run" she yelled

The girls ran out of the Brook Gate Shopping plaza. They walked along Smith Rd until they came upon Brook Park the girls decided to crash there for the night. There were a lot of homeless people also sleeping along the benches, so the girls found a big tree in the middle of the park to bundle up against to get some rest. Cynthia stayed woke while the others slept when she noticed Diamond panting in her sleep {I'm going to kill you; I'm going to kill you"

"Hey, wake up it's a dream" Cynthia said

Diamond jumped out of her sleep breathing heavily

"You're ok it was just a dream"

Diamond looked her in her eyes" No it was a nightmare and yes I am going to kill him"

"Kill who?" Cynthia asked

"BEAST! My Father"

Chapter 11 (The gall arise triggering a heart rates uncontrollable pulsates) an in-depth focus will never lose concentration, when there's a start there almost always has to be a finish {**VEHEMENT**}

2 Weeks later

"Diamond wake up" Tauti said tapping her leg. Diamond refused the hospital since she's been in Virginia but she wasn't in the greatest shape when she got there. Tauti called in a close friend who happened to be a doctor in the community to check on her when she realized she wasn't getting any better. When Diamond opened her eyes she notices a strange man standing at the end of the bed. Surprised by his presence she jumped up.

"Whoa relax Diamond it's ok! This is a good friend of mine and he's also a doctor I would really feel a lot better if you were to just let him check you out to make sure everything is ok with you. You were in bad shape when I picked you girls up and nothing seems to be changing for you. You're always sleeping won't eat child you look like you're just withering away. Can he at least make sure you don't have any infections? I won't leave I'll be right here with you. Tauti said

"Where's Nola or Cynthia" Diamond asked

"They are right in the living room"

"I checked everyone out if you feel the least bit of discomfort just tell me and I'll stop you can trust me" Dr. Pinchbeck interrupted

Diamond was still in a lot of pain. She hated using the bathroom because it burned so bad; she knew she needed this doctor so she accepted the help. The doctor advised her of every step that would take place and slowly walked her through the prepping process.

"Ok I'm sorry to do this but I'm going to have to take a look" he said pointing to her nightgown

Diamond looked at Tauti who nodded her head with approval. She laid back and pulled up her nightgown and pulled down her underwear. He observed the bruising of her inner thigh and cuts leading to her vagina opening.

"Can you now open your legs for me?"

Diamond did as the doctor instructed

"Wow I'm so sorry this happen to you. The swelling had gone down a little, but it cuts and brush burns had gotten infected. Diamond I'm going to place my finger on you gently just to see if there's any inner bruising, but it will be uncomfortable and possibly hurt a bit ok"

"Ok" she whispered

The doctor took his finger and inserted it gently inside her to feel around for any lumps or bruises. Everything seems normal but the discharge on his finger was a clumpy green and had a fish odor. He pulled out a few swabs to and took samples to take back to the lab.

"Ok Diamond, how has urinating been lately for you?"

"It burns really bad and hurt my stomach I don't wipe either I sit until it dries" Diamond said

"I understand your cuts are infected which is causing you external burn and I think you may have a urinary infection and possibly more. I'm going to need a urine sample if u can. I know it's painful but just a little if you can. I can also give you something for the pain I'm pretty sure I know what infections you have. All curable so that's a good thing. I can get these samples over to the lab today and try to get them back to you tomorrow evening if that's ok Tauti" Dr. Pinchbeck said

"Yes, that would be great whatever will help right Diamond"

Diamond glared out the window not saying anything. She climbed out of bed and went into the bathroom with the small cup. She sat on the toilet placing the cup close to catch the urine. As she tried to push, she cried from the pain. She managed to get just enough out but there was blood mixed with her urine this time.

"Tauti she seems mighty young and I won't ask questions but I will let you know she's carrying a STD. It's either gonorrhea or Chlamydia from the signs of her discharge and I'm pretty sure she has a urinary tract/ or bladder infection which is causing the discomfort when she urinates. She was brutally assaulted and I know your citizenship status so I'm assuming she's in the same boat. I won't contact the authorities but this is awful she doesn't look any older than 9"

"Well I just want to thank you for everything including being discreet but I can't answer anything it's a complicated situation as you can see" she replied

Diamond exited the bathroom and handed him the cup, "that's all I could do" she said lying back down

"Thank you Diamond! I'm going to get you the medications ASAP. Tahiti u can pick them up right away that will cure up all that pain. But in the mean time here are a few pain relievers that will help with the pain during urination for now and I'll be in touch with the results"

"Thank you, Diamond I'll get the girls for you and walk you out Doc"

Tahiti walked the doctor out and advised the girls Diamond was awake. Nola ran into the room with the laptop.

"Look at this" she pulled up the Cleveland news clip Human Trafficking Ring found 43 missing children Friday afternoon. 1black unidentified male and 1 black unidentified female were dead on arrival, along with 3 suspect's 43-year-old Drew Zion Lee who goes by Druzy from Youngstown. 26 years old Derek Nichols who goes by Raw from Youngstown and a Hector Rodriquez who's also been a person of interest in several unsolved trafficking rings across the East Coast. The three are currently being held in the Cleveland County jail with 1 million dollar bonds each.

"He got away; Beast got away" Diamond yelled kicking the laptop

"I'm sorry, I been watching waiting to see if anything changed and nothing he's gone. Just let the past be the past we can all start over Aunt Tauti don't mind you staying awhile" Nola said

"And then what? Get comfortable until she gets tired and give me up too" Diamond said

"No! It not even like that" The other girls heard the 2 yelling and ran in.

"What's going on, Cynthia asked picking up the laptop. Oh you seen it I'm so sorry"

"Hey girls, so there's a Fish fry going on today and you all been cooped up in this house so I thought maybe you all might want to go. Diamond you think you up for it. That pill should work in no time" Tauti walked in interrupting

"Uh auntie I don't think she's up to it"

"No, its fine I'll go, I'm feeling a little better already" Diamond replied

"Ok good, well it starts at 4 you all take turns showering. Good thing I'm just an itty bitty huh I'm sure all you girls can fit everything in my closet she laughed. Ill grab a few things and you girls can pick out what you want. Now I want you girls to remember you can't talk about anything that has happen to any of you. You girls are my brother daughters here to visit that's it ok? And Diamond are you sure you're ok?"

"Still a little sore but I'll be ok. I want to get some fresh air" she replied

"Ok baby... Well get showered at ill find you all some clothes" Tahiti left the girls and went to find each of them clothes to wear while they all showered.

The fish fry was being run by Pastor Johnson and his wife Sister Johnson. They did a lot of giving back to the community by hosting anti- drug and gun rally's, block parties and fish fry's trying to bring everybody together. Pastor Johnson also recently remodeled Macedonia Baptist church and is always looking to welcome new comers. Tauti would show her face here and there but was never interested in becoming a member of the church. The fish fry was in the memory of his late son Tyrone Johnson who was murdered leaving a party in Richmond two Days before his 17st birthday. Tyrone and Tyrek were twins and known jack boys in the Virginia. Pastor Johnson tried his hardest to lead the boys down a different path, but nothing helped until the death of Tyrone. Tyrek learned quick that the fast life didn't show no love or mercy. So he changed his life around and became an active member of Macedonia church.

"You girls already to go" Tauti asked putting on her earrings

"Is it like church people preaching in our ear cause if so, I'll stay here" Cynthia said

"Well what's wrong with hearing a good word or two? After all you all been through maybe you should take some of it in"

"I aint no charity case, I rather not" Déjà responded

"Well no it isn't! It's just the people in the community coming together eating drinking dancing and having fun which you could all use. I understand you've been through a lot, but you don't have to be so shut down. Everyone doesn't want to hurt you. I'm just trying to show you that. It takes baby steps, but you have to start somewhere" Tauti said

"Well I want to go! Déjà and Nola said me too Diamond said

"Alright then let's go"

The girls all jumped in Tauti s car. Diamond rolled down the window closed her eyes and just let the air hit her face. She replayed Beast face in her head and it only angered her. She could still smell him; hear his voice even envision his smug grin. She knew she would see him again real soon but for now she'll get comfy, get healthy then plan her next move.

Tauti pulled up into Macedonia parking lot that was full of happy people enjoying life. The sisters instantly got excited but things like this were nothing new to Diamond. Back when Bam was alive he made sure she had the full experience of what fun was for a child. Cynthia Nola and Déjà on the other hand have never had the privilege of enjoying things like this.

"Well what you girls waiting on" Tauti said

"Well should we just go?" Nola asked

"Well yes all are welcome but come on I'll break the ice for you all" Tauti said getting out the car. The girls followed her over to Sister Johnson

"Well hello gorgeous how are you" Tauti said

"Oh, hey honey I'm just fine and yourself? And who are these gorgeous young ladies looking like your sisters" Sister Johnson laughed

"Well this is Cynthia, Nola, Diamond and Déjà my nieces who came to visit me for a while"

"Well it's nice to meet all of you; you're welcome to any food or beverages you like. We have games over there, there's a park and a variety of different things to do. Everyone is friendly so don't be shy alright now"

The girls nodded and smiled. Diamond looked around when she spotted a table with Mountain Dew soda on it which was her favorite. "I'm getting a soda" she said

"I'll come with you" Nola said

"Well girls I'm going to make my rounds, but I'll be close if you need me" Tauti said walking away. The girls split up and walked around to get a feel for the place.

"This is pretty cool I've never been to nothing like this before" Nola said drinking her soda

"I've been to all types of stuff like this and church people are worse than regular people. All they do is talk about you then smile in your face then blame it on god. Bam taught me never to trust them" Diamond said

"Well Bam not here and who's to say he wasn't lying. You couldn't really trust him either right"

Diamond cut her eyes but realized she was possibly right. The one person she loved the most and only person that she thought loved her wasn't who he said he was. How could she trust anybody again? She thought

"You might be right, but everybody lies at one point or another right" Diamond said walking away"

She walked into Macedonia church just to look around. It was big with semicircular decorative wall surface over the entrance. Large vaulted space to draw attentions to the heavens that were placed along the ceilings. Angels floated side by side on the walls with rows that seem like they went forever and ever. Diamond walked down the main isle and sat down in the 13th row. She just sat there enjoying the silence and peace that she wanted so bad when she heard voices coming from the back. She got up and crept to the back where she seen 2 bodies intertwining with one another outside of what looked like the pastor's office. She got a little closer and noticed Tauti and Pastor Johnson kissing while he had his hands up her skirt. Diamonds eyes widened in shock, she slowly backed out of the hall without being seen. Diamond got halfway down the aisle when she was stopped by an unknown girl.

"Hey, have you seen my daddy?"

"Umm I don't know who that is" Diamond said walking past her

"Oh, I'm sorry Pastor Johnson; I'm Tory his daughter momma said he went to grab papers thought you may have seen him. What's your name?"

"I'm Diamond. I think I seen him leaving out a few seconds ago" Diamond mumbled looking back towards the office.

"Hey, I thought I heard voices" Tauti said running out fixing her blouse. "Hello Miss Tory, how are you today?"

"I'm good Momma just sent me in to find my daddy"

"Oh, yea he's back in his office typing up something or another. I'm sure he'll be out soon. I heard everybody was about to do the potato sack races girls lets go that should be fun" she said taking focus away from the pastor.

"Oh yes it's so fun Diamond come on you can be my partner" Tory said grabbing Diamonds hand. Diamond looked back at Tauti then followed Tory to the sack races.

"You're new around here huh?"

"Wouldn't say new I don't plan to be here that long" Diamond responded
"Well that's too bad I would love a new friend everyone thinks I'm weird because I'm the pastor's daughter"

"Everyone that thought I might have been weird is dead"
"What!"

"Nothing it doesn't matter. Why do people think your weird? You're clothes are fancy you got that long white girl hair your pretty"

"I really don't know honestly I try to be pretty cool but it freak people out"

"I guess" Diamond responded

"Do you mind if I ask you something! Do you believe in God? He can walk you out of whatever trouble you may be in whether it's internal or ext."

"Yea I see why people think you're weird. You Jesus freaks just love cramming how good god is. If he was so good, I wouldn't be here in this strange place with you strange people. I would have a mom and a dad that loved me."

"Family isn't always blood and God is real if you let him be" Tory preached

"Yea thanks but no thanks let's just play the game" Diamond said becoming annoyed. The girls all took turn racing and surprisingly they had a good time. The day almost made them forgot about the nightmare they had encountered.

"Hey Diamond, would you like to stay over my house, I can ask my mom"

"I don't think that's a good idea"

"Come on why not" Tory plead

"I'll ask if it's alright I guess "Diamond said

"Ok come on let's go" The 2 girls ran over to Tauti who was sitting with Cynthia Déjà and Nola.

"Hey Ms. Tauti, is it ok if Diamond stays over?"

"Oh, looky looky Diamond got a new bff I see" Nola said sarcastically jokingly

"Well I'm not sure is it ok with your parents? Diamond are you feeling ok everywhere. I remember your stomach wasn't the best earlier.

"It's ok now but maybe I should wait a few more days before I go anywhere else Tory we can exchange numbers and maybe next weekend I should be here awhile I think"

"Ok fine 540-367-3245 call me ok you were so fun"

"Ok I will" she smiled Tory ran off and Diamond stayed seeing that it was getting dark. The girls gave her mean looks as she sat next them. Tauti packed it up and the girls headed home. No one said anything to each other in the car ride.

"So, did everybody enjoy themselves Diamond I know you did every time I looked up you and Miss Tory was somewhere laughing that was great to see after so much you've been through."

"Yea I had a good time! I see you had a good time to the preacher really likes you around huh"

Tauti looked at her through her rear-view Diamond didn't blink "Oh yeah me and the Pastor been good friends for years and Sister Johnson"

Diamond rolled her eyes and looked out the window. Nola leaned over to Diamonds ear and whispered {now you a goody two shoes bitch huh} Diamond didn't flinch or react to her comment she stared out the window following the full moon lost in thought. They arrived at the house the girls jumped out and ran in the house Diamond was last out the car.

"Now Diamond I don't know what you think you saw but you didn't see it ok. I would hate for you to end up on the streets by yourself again" Tauti said noticing Dr. Pinchbeck waiting on the porch. "Doctor is everything ok" she said getting out the car

"Hey Tauti, sorry I know it's kind of late but when I got the results I wanted to come right over. I even stopped and grabbed the medicine for her."

Diamond got out the car and walked towards him "Well what is it"

"Well it's just as I thought you have Chlamydia. It's a bacterial infection transmitted through sexual contact. It can be cured but if left untreated can cause very unpleasant circumstances. Also, you have a UTI Urinary Tract infection which is the reason for the pain while urinating which goes hand in hand with the STD and HPV infection. I'm so sorry for this but I'm glad we caught it. The HPV has no treatment so we will just have to keep an eye on it every 6 months to a year until your body defeats it on its own which it usually does. Any questions so far?"

"No, now what" Diamond said bluntly

"Well you just take all these pills together and you should be fine by the morning. Make sure you eat something to avoid an upset stomach, you still may feel a little icky at first but it will do the trick. Are you sure you don't have anything to ask me I know this is a lot of information for someone your age especially due to the situation?"

"Nope eat, pop the pills and its over noted. Is that it Doc"

"No that about does it. Tauti just keep an eye on her make sure she drinks plenty of fluids ok"

Diamond grabbed the prescription bag and walked in the house. Cynthia and Nola yelled uppity bitch think she got friends now as she walked past. Diamond ignored them grabbed her towel walked into the bathroom and locked the door. She ran the shower on the hottest temperature and watched herself in the mirror until the glass fogged as she silently cried.

Chapter 12 (A ruptured or frazzled emotion can awaken a sleeping Beast) you can turn your back or even close your eyes, but you don't always need vision to see {**WASPISH**}

"Hello, can I speak to Tory" Diamond said nervously from the other end of the phone

"One second may I ask whose calling" Tyrek responded

"This is Diamond" ok one second Tory get the phone he yelled

"Hello" Tory said

"Umm hi this is Diamond"

"Oh yes Diamond hey, how are you? I wasn't sure you would call but God kept sending me little hints.

"God yea sure so what's up" she asked watching to make sure no one came in the room

"Nothing much just got done eating dinner its pizza Fridays, getting ready to watch a movie. Why did you want to come over I could use some company? Tyrek's friends are all downstairs and mom and dad are gone until who knows so I'm just sitting here blah you know"

"Well I'm going to get Tauti to drop me off if that's ok"

"Really! She said excitingly Yes, I'll text them right now and tell them! We said a prayer for you the other day us Christians feel certain vibes from people I know you sure could use it even if you don't need it it's always good to have." Tory preached

"Listen if I come over we're not going do this whole god thing all night right. I'm not against it but I'd just rather not. I could use a friend that's all and apparently so could you so can we just be normal kids for a night I been through enough in this house with these chicks."

"Oh ok I'll try my best. Ill text them now and tell them you're coming see you soon" Tory said before hanging up.

Since the first day Diamond met Tory the girls no longer spoke to her as if she didn't have enough on her plate already. Tory was light skinned tall long jet black hair and the pastors daughter so befriending her was a huge snob alert in the eyes of those who weren't her friend. Diamond walked in the room where everyone was watching Law & Order

"Hey Tauti can you drive me to Pastor Johnsons house" Diamond asked with her head down avoiding eye contact with Nola.

"Uh sure I can, did you get the ok to come over"

"Yes, I did"

"Ok well go get your thing s together I'm glad you made a new friend" Tauti said with a fake grin

Diamond ran upstairs to gather her overnight bag when she heard multiple steps climbing the stairs.

"Dumb bitch don't think you special, you're still a little nasty trash dumpster" Déjà said knocking her clothes out her hand

"Why are you like this to me? I did nothing wrong. We all had messed up things happen to us I'm just trying to get back to normal. What's wrong with that? We're all still friends"

"You will never be normal; your own daddy fucked you! Your garbage, don't forget that no matter what church people you sit under." Cynthia and Nola stood with a huge grin on their face. Diamond bent over to pick her things up from the floor and put them in her bag grabbing the razor blade she kept next to the nightstand.

"Garbage huh, she whispered charging Cynthia putting the blade to her throat. Shut up all of you or Ill cut her! The 3 silenced see I've been trying to be very patient with you fucking cunts. Hiding my tears, biting my tongue because right now I need this place but my patience is almost gone and I have nothing to lose at this point. Cynthia's neck began to bleed

"You're hurting me" Cynthia said

"I'm hurting you! Listen here all of you stay out my way I plan to be out of here sooner than later but until then leave me the fuck alone! I've already killed twice she said looking in her eyes and I have no problem adding bodies"

"Diamond is you ready" Tauti yelled from the bottom of the steps. Diamond paused for a second not taking her eyes off Cynthia then she removed the blade from her neck, "yes ma'am here I come" The 2 girls rushed to Cynthia placing a napkin around the small cut on her neck.

"Oh, I will be back so say something if you want I'll get to you one way or another. Just stay out my hair and I'll stay out of yours until I'm out of here for good" Diamond said grabbing her things and walking out the room.

"Crazy bitch Déjà whispered are you ok?" Cynthia nodded still frightened as they watched Diamond leave the house.

Tauti drove in silence not sure what of what to say to Diamond especially since she knew she was having an affair with Pastor Johnson but tried to make small talk anyway.

"So, this should be exciting huh meeting new people venturing off getting back to life"

"Yea I'm excited she's seems cool. So does Sister Johnson and Pastor Johnson but you knew that already right" Diamond said

"Now look don't you go spreading any rumors what you think you saw you didn't and we need to keep it that way especially since your living under my roof rent free not being my responsibility and all."

"Tauti relax no need for the idle threats we both know you need your secret to stay a secret and I need a place to stay for now at least. Don't worry I'll be out your hair and your secret is safe unless someone else knows your boning the pastor."

"Watch your mouth young lady, what's gotten into you" Tauti asked appalled

"Honestly your nieces are driving me crazy as if I haven't been through enough all because I want to make friends with someone other than them. I guess I shouldn't have expected so much.

"Everybody deals differently Diamond you can't fault or blame them for their actions they're victims like you" Tauti said pulling up to the pastor's house

"I don't want to stay a victim that's the difference I just want to move on. Thank you for the ride my lips are sealed" Diamond said getting out the car

"Have fun call me when you're ready tomorrow" Tauti yelled driving off. Tory stood at the door waiting for Diamond to reach the top step. Her home looked like something off the movies.

"Hey Diamond, I'm so happy you're here let me take your stuff! Tyrek my company is here dad said its fine" Tory yelled. Tyrek walked out the kitchen

"Hello nice to meet you, there's still pizza left in the kitchen if you want help yourself"

"We'll come back let me give you the tour" Tory said excitingly the stairs lead to the second floor of the house. There were 5 bedrooms one office and an exercise room. Each bedroom had its own bathroom.

"This is my room! I never have company, but my parents got me a guest bed just in case so it's like it's yours since you're the first to sleep in it."

"This house is amazing wow" Diamond said looking around who all lives here

"Well it's me my parents and brother but we always have visitors coming to the church, so we have guest rooms for everyone. Guess what else we have... A pool! Want to go?" Flash backs of the last time she swam with Mika flashed before her eyes she paused

"Diamond! Hello Diamond, you there" Tory asked

"Oh, sorry she grinned I don't have a suit"

"Silly we have tons! Come on let's go it's so warm too"

Tory walked Diamond around the rest of the house last stop was the pool room. Tory and Diamond changed into their suits. Diamond still had visible bruising on her inner thighs, so she tried to cover up with her towel. When she left the dressing room Tory was already in the water

"Come on in its great" she yelled Diamond smiled, threw her towel and jumped in. The water in her hair all over her body felt like the cleanse she needed it was so refreshing. She floated along the bottom of the 5ft for what seemed an eternity. Bam's face was all she could see with her eyes closed under water. She rushed to the surface when she realized she was running out of air. Tory swam from the 12th feet to meet her in the 5ft.

"It looked like you needed that" Tory joked

"Oh, sorry been awhile since I swam"

"What happen to your legs? It looks painful. Sorry you don't have to answer that if you don't want"

Diamond paused unsure if she should tell her what really happen or make up a lie

"I was hurt by someone" Diamond said

"Hurt you like what? Especially in between your legs! Oh my god I'm sorry" Tory said when she realized where the conversation was going. There was an awkward silence between the 2. Diamond kicked her feet in the water while Tory just looked at her trying to hold back tears.

"Don't feel sorry for me you don't even know the story"

"God should've protected you"

"God ha what a joke, I told you our gods are different and so is our life so stop trying to make everything work the same it doesn't and I'm ok with that. I get hurt but don't stay hurt his days are marked"

"You know who did this to you?" Tory asking surprisingly

"Yup my father

"YOU'RE FATHER, Jesus pave away to bring serenity to Diamond dear God she needs it more now than ever!" Tory yelled

"STOP I don't need this just be the friend you wanted in me I'll be fine trust me"

"Can I just ask one more thing?"

"What's that's"

"Are you ok? Tory asked

Diamond sat and looked away for a while NO I'm upset, and I want revenge and I plan to get it by any means necessary using whoever and whatever to do so! I plan to kill him not saying today or tomorrow but I promise you he will die"

"Lord Jesus Diamond I don't know much about you but since the day I met you I knew there was something about you. God sent me to save you please let me. Just one Sunday come to church and listen to his word it works he speaks to you through other Christians trust me. Just stay the whole weekend instead of going home tomorrow I promise you won't regret it. Have you ever been horseback riding?"

Horseback riding she laughed what's that have to do with God" Diamond asked

"Nothing that's just on the list of things to do tomorrow you're welcome to join"

"You do a lot of white people stuff huh" they laughed

The 2 continued to swim laughing and enjoying each other. Diamond put her guard down a little bit and enjoyed just being a kid for a while. After swimming they grabbed some more pizza and watched movies until they fell asleep in the theatre room.

"Somebody had fun last night; Sister Johnson said opening the blinds in the theatre room Hello Diamond good to see you again you have no idea how excited she was when you called"

"Mom," Tory said"

"I'm sorry but you were I'm just glad you girls had fun I see you used the pool when's the last time you swam Tor"

"Diamond come on we can go to my room" Tory said

"Well Horseback riding starts at 2 is she staying or leaving"

"I'm staying Mrs. Johnson" Diamond said

"Oh, call me Carla and that's great have you been horseback riding before if not just know you'll love it"

"I look forward to it" Diamond said walking away. She entered the kitchen and noticed Pastor Johnson drinking his coffee.

"Hello and who are you" he asked

"I'm Diamond Tory's friend Tauti's niece, you do remember Tauti right? She said giving him the eye. The pastor looked around to make sure no one noticed her gesture.

"Oh yes Tauti sure, how is she by the way"

"Hmmm I'm sure you know the same as me Pastor"

The pastor looked confused "I don't know what you think you know but your imagination seems to be getting the best of you" he stuttered

"Imagination, yup guess your right imagination"

"Hey daddy so you met Diamond" Tory interrupted is it ok if she stays until tomorrow to go to church with us please" she begged

"Uh sure why not I guess that should be ok"

"Ok were going to get dressed for Horseback riding, Tory said dragging Diamond out the room. Tory let Diamond borrow some of her clothes that were more suitable for horseback riding. They wore matching cowboy hats and boots. Sister Johnson accompanied the 2 while the pastor stayed back. When they arrived at the stables it began to rain but stopped suddenly. Diamond had never ridden a horse before but hopped on anxious to get a feel for it. The instructor advised everyone to stay in line one horse after another to follow him up the trail. Diamond watched as Tory guided her horse and kicked when she wanted to go faster. She caught on to the technique and kicked the horse to speed up. The horse began to run in full speed causing the other horses to follow. Yay she screamed encouraging the horse to go faster as she fled through the trail now leaving all the other horses behind. She tried to pull on the rope to get him to slow down but she wasn't strong enough, so he didn't. Getting closer to the woods she panicked after trying to stop him she jumped off the horse landing on her right arm she screamed in pain. The instructor finally caught up to her screaming on the ground holding her arm. He hoped off the horse and picked her up.

"Jesus Diamond is you okay, I told you to slow down" Tory said Diamond just cried in pain

"I think her arm is broken she may need to go to the hospital!"

"No Diamond yelled I'll be fine" she said trying to gain strength in her arm to prove her point.

"It looks bad! Dislocated bad! Are you sure? Let's go show momma" Tory said?

The girls walked back to the stables while the instructor led the rest of his class up the trails in the woods. Diamond fought so hard to hold back tears, but her arm was in agonizing pain. Once they got back to the stables Sister Johnson got Diamond back to the car and to her house to see if ice and a sling would do the trick. She also called Tauti to inform her of the situation.

"Hey Tauti, this is Clara Johnson"

"Hello" she said nervously

"Well we took the girls horseback riding today and Diamond your little daredevil decided she wanted to play cowboys and Indians. The poor child fell of the horse and sprained her arm bad. There's a lot of bruising and swelling but it looks like the ice is working for now and I put it in a sling, but she doesn't want to go to the hospital. I thought maybe you can convince her.

"That poor child dreads the hospital ever since she was little if she's not literally dying you couldn't force her to go. Is she ok?" Tauti asked

"Well for now she's sitting here with an ice pack and the swelling is going down, but she can barely move it.

"Okay well let her let it heal if it doesn't get better call me I'll come get her and take her"

"Alright I'll keep you posted" Sister Johnson said before hanging up. Ok well Tauti said to let it soak and keep an eye on it but if it doesn't get better she'll have no choice but to take you ok Diamond."

"Okay" she said

Sister Johnson left the living room while the girls sat and watched TV for a while. Tory couldn't help but stare at Diamond confused but every time Diamond would catch her she would look away.

"What you keep looking at me like that for" Diamond asked

"Are you trying to kill yourself" Tory asked

"What" she laughed

"I'm not joking; the lord has been giving me so many signs that something is wrong with you. I watched you almost not come up when we were in the pool. Then I watched you spiral out of control almost causing that horse to kill you on purpose! It almost makes me wonder if you have some sort of death wish. Or maybe you are the devil"

"You're getting weird on me again. I don't want to kill myself I'm just learning to enjoy my fear it's making me stronger! You know preparing me."

"Preparing you for what?"

"Don't ask questions you don't want the answer to Tory"

"No I do want the answer"

"I want revenge!"

"Revenge is nothing more than unreleased hate let it go let god heal you"

"Right, god tomorrow at church remember" she responded sarcastically

Sunday Morning

"Girls get up were all running late. Your father can't miss this 9 o'clock sermon that's where most of the donations come from" Sister Johnson screamed waking Diamond and Tory up. The clock read 834am which left enough time to do absolutely nothing, but Diamond and Tory shuffled around getting dressed to make it on time. The ice worked on Diamond arm, but it was still sore, so she kept the sling on. Tory gave her a dress to wear because she had only brought some faded denim jeans and a crop top Tauti gave her. The family gathered in the car and rushed to church making it at exactly 9 o'clock.

"Ok girls go in and find a seat" she advised. Tory guided Diamond to the second row but she declined. "I'm sitting in the back I don't know these people"

"But we won't get a good view of daddy" Tory responded

"You stay then, Diamond said walking away. She found a seat in the second to last row of the church. 2 older woman and 3 kids were in the same row with her, but she paid them no mind. She couldn't believe how many people attend churches it was over 400 people there.

"Welcome welcome old comers and new comers to Macedonia Baptist church. I'm not going to give it to you sweet today okay because this morning I woke up with something heavy on my heart. I got up and I heard that voice and you know who it was! God! It was god himself and he said Pastor let's learn a little bit more about forgiveness. Amen {Amen} church people ranted See just like most of you I have sinned more than once I can guarantee but I'm able to stand here in front of all of you and give you my truth through his word you know why? Because god forgives all his children .We were put here to sin to live but to learn. To let hurt go to go through it and to forgive those who may have hurt us Amen

"Amen" the lady shouted out sitting next to Diamond

His words began to tune out to her because there was no such thing as forgiveness in hers eyes she wants revenge. She watched as everybody held onto to every word the Pastor had spoken although he was a dishonest person himself. And Sister Johnson who sat right next to him in the pulpit with no idea enraged her.

"Alright now, were going to take this time to pass around the collection plate. It's not obligation to anyone of course but it's our way of giving back to god. Last Sunday we manage to bring in 3600 dollars to Jesus Amen. There's one coming down the right hand side and the left just take some time out and give what you" Pastor Johnson expressed.

Diamond was new to the church system and how everything worked but she watched carefully realizing everyone was putting money on a plate and passing it around. Jackpot she thought! She watched as it reached her row, the lady with the 2 children pulled out 2 hundred dollar bills and 3 fifty dollar bills and placed them on the plate and passed it to Diamond. She took a second to look at all the money and her surroundings to see if anyone was watching her. When she realized no one was looking she reached in her pocket as if she was pulling out money and grabbed the 2 hundred dollar bills and 1 50 dollar bill on top of the plate and passed it to the row behind her. She slowly put the money in her arm sling.

"I saw that! That's god's money" Tory whispered standing behind her causing Diamond to Jump. She jumped up and pulled Tory into the hallway.
"Is there going to be a problem Tory"

"Jesus is watching he's always watching"

"Was he watching when" she paused

"What why won't you talk to someone if not me God"

"Listen Tory I have a plan and I'm sticking to it God will understand. You just keep your fucking mouth shut and let me handle my business and we will be just fine ok"

"Ok! Tory said frightened wait where are you going?" she yelled

"I'll find my own way home" Diamond yelled walking out the church. She wasn't familiar with the area she was in but ran into Tyrek Tory's brother standing on the side of the church sneaking a cigarette.

"Now what would god think" Diamond joked

Tyrek frighteningly threw the cigarette "Oh it's just you, girl you scared me! Last thing I need is one of these holier than thou folks telling my father anything else"

"I'm just happy you're not throwing holy water at me like your parents and sister. It can't really be that great to be a Christian if you got to sneak to be human" Diamond stressed

"Between me and you I'm just trying to stay in my father's good grace to keep my ass out the streets. Me and my brother were in some heavy shit back in the day but now I'm strictly into this computer shit. Call it geeky but you'd be surprised at what I've taught myself in such little time. Keep that between me and you though" he laughed looking around

"Heavy shit huh. You could be of good use to me" she said giving him the eye

"How old are you anyway you can't be no older than what a good 12 13 if that"

"What different does it make? I've probably lived the life of a 31 year old man age can't change that"

"Yea you can say that again, he said relighting his cigarette

"Can I ask you a question?"

"Yea what's up?"

"How much would you charge to get me some information on someone?"

"Someone like?"

"That doesn't matter at the moment, but I want information and ongoing information until I'm ready to use the information" Diamond expressed

"Well you talking money so you got my attention but where would you get the type of money I would need to find out this information?"

"First things first can you do it?"

"Well to answer your question little one, I have access to any and every one. Full data whether its background, credit, addresses social security I can find out what color draws somebody wearing all from that big ole fishbowl these folks called church. That data base is as good as the FBI if you feel what I'm saying. I can hack security cameras hell I can unlock the front the just from sitting at a computer" He said confidently

"Well here's 250 dollars. That's my down payment and I have more where that came from"

"Oh yea 250 he counted and what little boy broke your heart? Who you need me to check up on" he joked?

"That would be funny if I found it to be, she said with a straight face. I don't need your humor I need your resources! That's my down payment do we have a deal" Tyrek straightened up his face when he seen how serious her face was

"Yeah does my sister know about this?"
"Like I said I need to do business, she's not quite business oriented like I need if you can understand"

"Oh I know. Who do you need info on?"
"That's something we can discuss at another time I just need you to know I'm serious. Once I give it to you I'll make sure you have a comfortable amount of money to do the things I need done Deal"

"Deal" Tyrek said recounting the money

"Good I'll be in touch" she said walking away

"Hold up where you walking to you need a ride or something? City bus be wiggly on Sundays

"Sure why not take me to Tauti's house please…

Chapter 13 (A mouse can move quickly past a scavenging bird of prey) Fear makes senses heighten, reflex sharper and focus scattered abroad leaving one undefeated {SAVAGE}

11 Sundays went by and Diamond made sure she attended every service. She rotated the seats she sat in but it was always somewhere close to the back where there were few people sitting in the same row as her and like clockwork when the collection plate got to her she would act like she was going in her purse this time dropping at least 10 dollars in while taking almost 500 dollars out then she would pass the plate along to the next row. She managed to accumulate 9700 dollars so far. Tory knew what she had going on but was so happy to have a friend that she ignored her sins and prayed for her. Diamond would stay over her house every Saturday night to make it to church Sunday morning. She even gave Tauti a few dollars to buy her different church dresses.

Cynthia and Nola manage to stay out of her way, but Déjà ran away with a white man she met online leaving a note for Tauti that she was in love. She couldn't report missing persons because she was here illegally. Her sisters were delirious believing that she found true love even though the info online about the man she had met disappeared no trace of either of them. Tauti enrolled Cynthia Diamond and Nola into school but Diamond never went and reminded Cynthia that she would slit her throat if she ever told. When the girls would get up to walk to school the girls would go left while Diamond went right.

She took her time learning the streets of VA with Tyrek's help. He would meet her most days at different spots and take her where ever she needed to go with a price of course.

"So, who run things around here" She asked

"Umm the police" he joked

"No, I mean who really run things around here? You keep showing me all these places but all I see is a bunch of runners who's the connect, you know the boss?" Tyrek looked at her confused

"Connect?!? What are you really trying to get yourself into?"

"I like to put faces with titles, titles with names, names with statue"

"Where and what the hell did you come from?" he asked seriously Diamond laughed

"Well there's a dude called P-Funk but he's big business I'm sure he had something to do with killing my brother. That's why I got out its too hot out here in these streets. I stay low and behind my tint. That dude is a monster and honestly I don't think you should even try to compare to whatever you think you may have had going on in your previous life"

"Don't think you know me! I'm not trying to compare just trying to find somebody to do my dirty work and it will work trust me! I mean look at you" she laughed

"All I'm doing is riding your little curious ass around you can't compare"

"Actually, she said pulling out 5000. It's time for you to do what I asked you a few months back remember" she said

"Not really! You only said you wanted me to look someone up"

"Not true what I said was look up and keep tabs on which mean when I ask for an update you have that info! I can ask Google for a look up this is 5000 dollars"

"Ok I'll do it he said looking at the money what do you want to know?"

"EVERYTHING"

"Ok who is it?"

"He goes by Beast he's from Youngstown Ohio. He's known so you have to do some research I want to know everything on him I don't have his real name"

"Ok and then what happens?" he asks

"I pay you more money to find and put my gun in his mouth" she smiled

"What!" he said

"I'll get out here. Let me know when you got something" Diamond said hopping out the car

"Wait is you serious" he laughed

"Tyrek if you only knew, she said slamming the door. Don't let me down find that info please" she replied before disappearing into the Italian bodega. Tyrek drove off intrigued. Diamond walked around the bodega to the deli. She ordered an Italian sausage and sauerkraut hoagie with a ginger ale and took it to the check out.

"Hey, you're Tauti s little girl" the clerk said Diamond smiled

"Yea she's my aunt"

"You tell her Tony said if she wants to keep her little pretty face the same she beta give me my money! He yelled grabbing her food off the counter. Now get your little boney ass out my store you're not welcome here" he yelled waving the broom

Diamond ran out of the store crashing into P-Funk causing him to drop his Colt 45.

"Damn what the fuck," he yelled

"I'm sorry, I'm sorry he's crazy" she panted

"It's cool little shorty is he fucking wit you! You lost or something?"

"No, I just wanted something to eat but he's upset at my auntie so I can't" He investigated the Bodega then looked back at the unknown girl frazzled and got upset.

"Come on shawty let's get you some food!" He said pulling out his gun. P-funk dragged Diamond back in the store waving his gun

"Sit your fat ass down, he yelled pointing his gun. Why the fuck aint you let her get nothing to eat you racist fuck"

"Funk, what the fuck are you doing! We just squashed the uptown down bottom war" The clerk expressed

"Fuck you, yea it was squashed until you threw one of my little young hungry black sisters on the streets! She had money too! Tell me why that happened!" he yelled Diamond stood next to him scared for her life

"Her aunt Tauti owes me money so she's not welcome here"

"Well now I'm involved these 2 different people this is a kid, get her a fucking sandwich. What kind did you have? He asked still waving his gun

"An Italian sausage hoagie with sauerkraut she mumbled"

"Make her a ma 'fucking sausage hoagie with sauerkraut nigga" the clerk did as he instructed. "What's your name youngin" P funk asked

"I'm Diamond"

"Diamond nice to meet you fucked up circumstances but nice to meet you just call me uncle P-Funk" Diamond had a look of shock on her face just the person she was trying to find.

"Nice to meet you Uncle P-funk" she said innocently. The bodega owner brought back her food and sat it on the counter.

"Lil Diamond, go get your food you good now" he instructed. Diamond looked him straight in the eye with a slight grin as she walked to the counter to get her food knowing that the gun was still pointed at him When she reached the counter she grabbed her food then reached in her pocket and pulled out the original money she was going to pay for the food and sat it on the counter.

"Can I have my change please" she asked politely still grinning. The bodega owner opened the register giving her exact change then backed up from the counter.

"See how smoothly that would've been if you wasn't being an asshole to my people. Nothing gets past me hear me nothing, so if a move need made from this fuck it! You know I'm always cocked and loaded ya dig" he said exiting the store with Diamond. "Come on youngin get off this block before he runs out bussing where you stay at? He asked. You Tauti's peoples that true?"

"Yea she's my aunt" she said being dragged behind P-funk

"Aunt, aint she Mexican or some shit" he said

"Yea some shit" she replied they both laughed

"You know Tauti be out here selling that twat stiffen niggaz that's why he mad. I'm sure you don't know what that mean but don't follow her footsteps she's bad news young buck. Come on though Ill drop you off up the way don't want you walking for real" he said

Diamond remember Tyrek saying P-funk was the one to see if you're looking for the boss and she already knew she got to him without getting to him how she wanted so her ducks were lining up perfectly. She let him drive her home acting completely ignorant to everything he spoke about Tauti or even the fact that she knew exactly who he was and already had a plan to use him for her revenge plot.

"Mr. thank you for standing up for me"

"Mister! No you can call me uncle P-funk"

"Oh yeah P-funk, can I call you sometime? Tauti is hardly home I'm new here I can use a new uncle"

"Ha he smiled I'm not the good uncle Diamond real shit I'm the bad guy and by that, I mean real bad guy"

"Well you don't seem too bad to me! You saved me from the bad guy. I Promise I won't be in your way I just don't know anyone here just thought it would be nice to find other people that's all" she said putting her head down"

P-Funk was known as the Crips God all through Fredericksburg. His father was a black panther killed by the cops when he was 7. Any drugs or guns that move he gave the ok and if he didn't there was trouble coming. He recently settled the turf war with the Italians, but he didn't stand for disrespect especially towards kids. His sister and 2 nieces were killed by her boyfriend all before turning the gun on himself. So, he walked around with a lot of animosity and anger.

"It cool Shawty here go my number, he said writing it down. If you ever in trouble hit me up real spill you sort of remind me of my sister when she was younger too"

"Oh, where is she now?" she asked

"She dead" he said. Diamond looked at the sadness in his response knowing he was exactly what she needed.

"Is the person that killed her dead too?"

"Yeah he is" he answered in satisfaction

"So the results didn't end so badly. I know it still don't bring them back but get them get you ya know. Thank you for the ride uncle P-funk drive safe" she said waving him off. Her comment caught him off guard, but he didn't think too much into it as he drove off. Diamond ran into the house to call Tyrek….

"Hello"

"Guess What" Diamond asked excited

"Diamond, get your little ass in here now" Tauti yelled

"Damn it I call you back Tyrek" she said hanging up. Diamond walked down the steps to Tauti holding a stash of her money and her book bag she had left on the floor.

"Where the hell did you get this money? Are you out here tricking" Tauti yelled?

"Tricking oh like you and Pastor Johnson or you and the guy at the Bodega"

"You watch your little fucking mouth I'm grown if that was the case that's my business either way you have no idea what you're talking about"

"Well he basically choked me for trying to buy a sandwich because you owe him money, I wonder why hmm" Diamond yelled back

"You know what you got 3 days to find you somewhere to stay I'm done"

"What! But where am I supposed to go, I need more time than that"

"I don't give a hell. 3 days and I want you gone" she said throwing her money back at her. You give me more problems than my own blood you got to go!

"Tauti please I'll pay you I have money!" she plead

"And what did you do for it, I came a long way and it took a lot to get back to my comfort level and settle into a new community. I don't need all this heat and attention you bring with your idle threats; this is my shit… 3 DAYS"

Diamond stood still as Tauti left the house. She had no idea what she would do or how she would do anything in 3 days with only 4700 to her name.

"Tough titty" Cynthia said joking walking pass her. Diamond noticed a glass ashtray sitting on the coffee table grabbed it and launched it hitting her in the middle of her forehead causing it to split open.

"Ouch Stop! She yelled grabbing her head dropping to the floor"

"Tough titty huh bitch, Diamond said walking pass as Nola ran out to help her

"What did you do? Nola yelled Diamond what the fuck"

Diamond went back to the room she stayed in and began to pack her bags completely zoning out the hysterical yelling going on in the other room amongst Cynthia and Nola. She had money with nowhere to go but she needed the church, so she decided to call Trek.

"Hey, I'm back I need you to come get me"

"Diamond what happen? What did you tell Tauti she told my dad she been seeing us together and think we are sleeping together or something?"

"What! That stupid bitch, just come get me I got some things to tell you"

"Man, I got to fall back for awhile. You know I can't afford any more trouble right now"

"We had a deal though" Diamond said

"And I plan to keep it just give me some time I'll talk to you later" Tyrek said hanging up.

"Fuck" she said to herself

"Diamond! What the fuck did you do?" Tauti yelled coming back in the house

Diamond ignored her continuing to pack knowing she had to get out of that house ASAP. After packing the rest of her things she made one more phone call

"Hello, a male voice answered

"Hi umm this is Diamond"

"Diamond, Diamond be more specific"

"Uncle P-Funk that is what you said was ok to call you. I got into some crazy things with Tauti and can't stay here she kicked me out. I have nowhere to go and you're the only other person I know in this town. Can I just stop pass maybe sleep on your couch a day or two until I figure things out? If not, I'll be on the streets and no one wants that. Well accept maybe Tauti"

P-funk paused for a minute: one because he was high 2 because he couldn't understand why Diamond felt comfortable enough to ask him for a favor like that after just meeting him

"You probably wondering why I would even ask such a thing, but you saved my life and stood up for me, so I know your heart is big despite your image. I need help can you do that for me?" she asked manipulating him

"I got you shorty my fault you just took me back for a second. No doubt I'm uncle P-Funk I love the kids. Can you get to me or you need me to get you? I got to tell you though my spots aint no places for a youngin like you, so you got to figure out your next move ASAP."

"Ok that's ok I got money saved just need a breath to figure things out"

"Cool I stay in Woodbridge. You know where that's at?"

"Yeah, what's the address"
"34983 Strew Ct"

"Ok thank you so much I promise I won't be a burden"

"Aright shawty, he said hanging up

Tauti ran up the steps "what the fuck is wrong with you! Why would you hit her like that she's going to need staples in her head because of you? I should call the fucking cops get the fuck out of my house. And leave my clothes"

"Oh, I left your raggedy clothes these are all my clothes and I'm leaving don't worry about that and I won't return promise thanks for nothing home wrecker" she said walking out of her house. Diamond was not too familiar with VA, but she knew of a jitney station that could get her to the address that P-Funk gave her. She walked 29th street with a book bag and a suitcase with all her things in it. She noticed as she walked past the church there was some activity going on inside, so she peeped her head in. Tory was leading a bible study for the younger age's boys and girls of the community along with a table in front of the door with care packages for the homeless. Even though

Diamond sympathized with Tory and even liked her she knew she could never live this type of life no matter how appealing it may have looked to her. As Diamond turned to exit the church, she spotted Tyrek walking in. She proceeded to keep walking past him, but he stalled walking slowly up the church steps allowing everyone to pass him by. Diamond kept walking while he called her name and ran up behind her.

"Didn't you hear me?"
"I thought you couldn't talk to me you know daddy's rules" she responded

"Don't take it personal but it was the truth"
"Then what are you talking for I'm good"
"It's not like Diamond chill, why you got all this stuff you going somewhere?"
"Well if you cared when I called you would've known Tauti kicked me out so I have to find somewhere to go"

"Damn why she do that?"
"She found some money and asked was I tricking, probably assuming it was with you since you're not allowed around me either"

"That's fucked up, did you tell Tory maybe she can ask if you can stay with us a few days or something"

"What makes you think your parents will want her around me either? It's cool I got a temporary spot until I figure things out"

"Where's that I thought you didn't know anybody here"
"That's what I was trying to tell you earlier dingbat. When

you dropped me off at that bodega all I did was go in there to buy a sand which and dude start tripping screaming about Tauti owing him money. I had nothing to do with anything and I had money to pay him. He tried to put his hands on me so out of nowhere you would never believe who showed up"

"Uh who superwoman" he joked

"No P-Funk"

Tyrek face instantly got serious, "ok what about him? He's bad news like I told you"
"That's just the thing I was explaining what happen and he turned into like Robocop or something all pro black queen type of stuff. He scared the shit out of the guy and he even gave me a ride. Told me to call him Uncle P-Funk" she smiled

"You're not listening this shit isn't cute he's the leader of the Crips he means business what you think he just going buy you juice boxes and new skirts for school. He will have you tricking or gang banging"

"Well I don't have a choice at this point. And I'm not there to stay I have a seed I want to plant. I know I can do it while staying low so why not. That's when you'll come in to play"

"What you mean into play! This aint a game Diamond! I'm not fucking with dude… that's part of the reason my brother dead. I'm saved now trying to do right:

"Do right? Well your people are peeking out the door wondering why you been out here so long Mr. Do right" Tyrek looked back nervously

"Listen I want to help you. I don't know your plan or what's the big secret vendetta but you cool and I want to help. But please don't get involved with his guy"

"Tyrek listen you're sweet and thank you for wanting to help but you already were going to help because we had a deal and I've been paying you. I only planned to let time pass by until I needed you which I will very soon so keep that same energy because your day will come as well sooner than you think. I have been around a lot of things in this small gap of life. I've got the knowledge so that makes me a real problem and now I'm not upset I'm pissed off and those that owe me will pay. Almost like the anger for your brother! One day that anger will unleash something that will be far out of your control it's in everyone. I just happen to find mine sooner than everyone else and I'm not ignoring it I'm going to use it.

"What! Who the hell are you for real! He asked in astonishment of the things she just said to him"

"I'll be in touch" Diamond said walking away

"Diamond, Diamond wait, he yelled"
"Go back to church and pray for me she yelled reaching the end of the street before disappearing.

Tyrek walked back into the church sitting in the back hoping no one noticed how long he was gone.

"Is u seeing Diamond? Don't you think you're a little old" Tory asked pooping out of the aisle

"Firstly, no I'm not dating her and I'm aware I'm older I just want to help her"

"She is stealing from the church you know"

"How do you know? I thought you were friends."

"God tell me everything, and now that I told you if you sit by and watch you're just as guilty" she said

"Tory stop spreading rumors if she's your friend that's not true now drop it" he said getting up going into his father's office.

Diamond reached the jitney stations but there weren't any cars available when she arrived

"How long before I can get a car" she asked the receptionist"

"Where you trying go"

"To wood bridge"

"Woodbridge! Good luck trying to find a driver who not scary enough to take the trip. They always robbing and shooting up something! Most the guys won't take it unless you are dropping some bank"

Diamond looked around at the empty station then outside realizing it was getting dark and she needed to get somewhere soon. "Bank huh, she said going in her bag.

Here goes 200 dollar bills can you make that call now PLEASE!"

The receptionist got on the phone; she advised one of the drivers that there was a female with bag possibly clothes as if she was kicked out or homeless who needed a ride to Woodbridge. She was alone and offering 200dollars upfront. Once she got the ok she advised Diamond to take a seat in the waiting room he would be about 20 minutes. She did as she was instructed as she waited for him to arrive. Love & Hip Hop was playing on the TV as she got comfortable. She dozed off for about 20 minutes before Nate showed up her driver.

"Are you waiting on a ride" he said tapping her shoulder

Diamond opened her eyes "Yeah I'm up"

"Let's go you going to Woodbridge right"

"Yeah, she said stretching and grabbing her bags

The 2 got in the car and merged onto 1-495

"So, where you going up Woodbridge you know that's a tough little spot right. You look young hope you are going to family's house" he said breaking the awkward silence

"Yeah I know my big brother live up there, I'm going to stay with him for a while."

"Oh yeah what's your brother name I may know him"

"Uh he goes by P- Funk"

"P-Funk what the Fu… he caught himself I mean no disrespect but he's one of the reasons that place went downhill. You know he's the ring leader in those parts"

"Yeah so what! I've heard that too its rumors you know he said this she said that. He's a good guy he gives back and protects woman and children. That's got to get him some point's right"

"Hmm if you say, so you are his niece so you haven't seen it all my best advice be careful. He's always surrounded around nothing but knuckleheads."

"Thanks, but I think I'll be ok" she said

"Alright well here's your stop up here on the left" he said pulling up to a blue house on the corner with a lot of men standing outside. Diamond got out the car grabbed her things and proceeded to walk into the house. She kept her head down as she walked but could feel everybody looking at her. When she reached the steps of the house a man stopped her...

"You lost or something" She looked at him unsure of what to say so she kept trying to walk. He jumped in front of her. You can't hear can I help you!" he said more aggressively

"I'm looking for P-Funk" she timidly responded

"That didn't answer my question!"

"Nigga get your dumb ass out the way and let her pass nigga" P-Funk yelled realizing it was Diamond. Come on shawty this way" he said waving towards the door.

Diamond continued to walk up the steps holding her things in her hands in relief. She entered the house that was full of marijuana smoke and loud music. To the right of her was 3 women dancing naked in the living room while men threw money at them. The left was a room with men yelling and throwing dice at the wall with money all over the floor. She caught eyes with the woman dancing; the 2 just looked at one another as she danced.

"This way shawty your room up here" P-Funk said breaking her attention. Diamond followed him up the steps. His house wasn't bad, but you can tell a woman's touch wasn't on it. There were clothes everywhere, no curtains up, and each room she passed had a box spring and mattress on the floor.

"Aright you can stay in this room, aint much but it works" he said. The room was the typical if you need somewhere to sleep here you go type of room. It had a bed a TV a dresser and closet.

"Thank you I really appreciate it and you don't have to worry about me I won't be any trouble. You don't have to pay for anything or feed me I got everything covered on my end. I just needed somewhere off the streets to figure things out"

"Listen, can I ask you something because I aint going front shawty you don't look like you can be any older than 12 maybe 13. So why are you out here dolo trying to handle or figure anything out?"

"Well I don't think age has nothing to do with anything. There's some people that are privileged to not have to figure things out on their own than there's others well there's me who do, simple as that." She said dropping her bag to the floor

"Yeah I hear you. While you're here keep your shit close by. I'll make sure don't anybody bother you, but I don't have control over people getting into your shit. You know niggaz will be niggaz feel me. I'm about to go back downstairs and I can't guarantee how long the turn up will last so listen, my room 2 doors down if it gets too loud and you want to go to sleep I got headphones on my dresser grab them put on your favorite song or some shit and try to fall asleep cool". He said

"Ok" she laughed I really appreciate this again"

"No doubt, he said leaving the room

Diamond looked around the room and glanced out the window watching as the guys in blue bandanas play fought and smoked weed. She laid down on the bed looking up at the ceiling as tears rolled down the side of her face.

"You can't get caught with crocodile's girl not around here. A random voice said. Diamond wiped her face and jumped up. Sorry if I scared you. I was up here on my way to the bathroom and noticed you laying there looking sad."

Diamond couldn't help but stare at the naked body of the woman standing in front of her. Her chocolate skin was glowing and her breast were so round a perky with piercing in them. Her abs looked like you can wash your jeans on them and she had the perfect landing strip underneath and heart tattoo that was centered in the middle of her pelvic bone.

"Hello anyone home" she said

"Oh, I'm sorry, didn't mean to stare" Diamond said

"It's ok I mean I am naked I'm sure this is a bit awkward for you. Diamond looked down to the floor. Girl you don't be shy it's not like we're both naked and trust me I have no problem showing off this body it's outstanding as you can see. She said smacking her ass… So, what's your name baby doll?'

"I'm Diamond"

"Really well surprisingly my name is Diamond too well my stage name anyway"

"Stage name?" she said confused

"Yes girl, what you don't think I just walk around dancing naked for nothing. Those moves you seen me making cost a pretty penny, she joked I'm a stripper"

"Oh, ok that makes sense now"

"You look familiar do we know each other?"

"I doubt it I'm not from VA" Diamond responded

"Do you go to Macedonia Church?"

Diamond looked up at her even more confused, you go to church?"

"Wow well that was judgmental! Yes, we can praise god and still be human"

"I wasn't trying to judge I was just shocked that's all. Yes, I have been going there for a few months now."

"Ok that's where I seen your little innocent eyes at then. Well I didn't mean to barge in you looked like you were getting ready to call it a night, so I'll go but it was nice meeting you hopefully I'll see you at church one of these weeks."

"Yeah you probably will thank you for stopping in and sorry for staring at your body" she joked

"No problem and it's my job so I'm used to it. I'm sure after all the testosterone you then walked past seeing and hearing females voice is a breath of fresh air. Well enjoy your night Diamond"

"You too Diamond"

"It's Tonya" she said winking an leaving the room

Diamond waited until she heard her leave the bathroom and go back downstairs to creep down the first 4 steps at the top of the stairwell to see if she could get a glimpse of the activity going on. She seen a guy passed out in the middle of the hallway looking like he wasn't breathing. 3 guys smoking out of what looked like a fish bowl while the others used a playing card to separate what looked like flour... Her view wasn't close enough to get a glimpse of Diamond dancing, so she crept 2 more steps down. Diamond was bent over the couch with her head in one of the guys lap while P-Funk was moving back and forth behind her. She moaned with pleasure every time she picked her head up. Diamond eyes go wide as she watched the sexual encounter amongst the 3 curious as to why that felt good to her but hurt so bad when it happened to her. The other girls danced all in the same room as if nothing was going on. Diamond began to feel a tingle in her panties as she watched and she could feel her pupils dilating.

"Aye who's this on the steps" a random voice yelled out. P-Funk looked back a seen Diamond sitting on the steps

"Take your little ass back upstairs" he yelled Diamond quickly ran back to her room closed the door jumped in the bed laughing before falling asleep.

Chapter 14 (If one does not lack perception one can manage a quick wit) Small ideas turn into goals or a mission don't forget that idea is what made the goal more achievable {COLLUSION}

"Now how in the fuck you expect me to beat you knowing damn well you only got one card left, you just going drop on me! I should've never taught you this damn game" P-Funk yelled out knowing he was about to lose another game of tonk to Diamond. She laughed in satisfaction knowing she was now 400 up more than the 5 dollar she put in. The two grew closer over the past 6 weeks they had spent together, and Diamond became a huge help round the house. Now the 5-bedroom single family house had curtains and a theme for the 2 bathrooms, one being blue seals and the other being ocean theme seeing as that blue was the only color she had to work with. Although nothing about P-funk's life changed he has had a different energy of hope having Diamond there.

"Yo what's lil shawty deal, I mean she shows up out of nowhere, she is taking all our money. She aint your kid sister or cousin like who the fuck is she for real." Monte said hitting his blunt. Monte was P-funks right hand man and cousin! Anything P couldn't handle or get to Monte did. Monte also became very fond of Diamond in these past 6 weeks never asking questions just taking P-Funks word which he stated was FAM. "I mean I'm not trying fuck up the good vibe Funk, but I been just as close to shawty as you have for about a good couple weeks and I know for a fact you can't have kids cause you my cousin.

And the damn stork bird aint just drop her off so the question remains my nigga {Who the fuck is she} no offense Diamond I love you to death from the few weeks I've known you but you see a lot of shit we into around here I need to make sure you aint the feds we got mad shit to lose"

Diamond looked up at him collecting her money in disbelief as she watched P-Funks face turn from laughter to suspicion. The 2 were both under the influence so she knew the situation could more than likely escalate if she doesn't make sense of the suspicions. She wanted to wait for the right time to, but it looks like that moment would have to do.

"That's a good fucking point" P-Funk said. You came out of nowhere basically showed on my door step! Are you 5.0?"

"What! 5.0 you met me at the bodega! You stopped me remember"

"How I know that wasn't a set up part of some plan the whole time? Your little pretty ass aint lost, you aint no runaway, aint nobody looking for you because I checked so, he said pulling out his gun who the fuck are you!!"

"OK aright! Please put the gun down and Il explain exactly who I am just get me a lap top and FUCK no I'm not the feds!" she explained

P-Funk sat the guns down and grabbed the laptop; although she was just a young girl the drugs convinced them she was part of the feds even though she's been living there for 6 weeks.

"Guys relax, I'll show you everything. She went to Cleveland news February 13th and pulled up the article stating huge trafficking ring.

"Take a look" she said sitting the laptop on the table. The two skimmed the story still not understanding her point.

"Ok I see some trafficking ring shit" Monte said

"Keep reading"

"Ok so it looks like the niggaz got caught! They arrested a few niggaz for it what's your point …"

"EXACTLY" she interrupted. A few but not the one that was supposed to be arrested he got away! I'm now realizing that was a good thing gives a chance to get to him. He's the problem and an issue in my life and I need him erased.

Monte and P- funk laughed. "Erased huh what you mean like dead? What he do hurt your feelings" he joked while Diamond kept a straight face

"Let me know when the jokes over" she responded

"Ok so what you know dude. You upset that he didn't get caught? Shawty do you know how many rings there are out there and how many people will continue to take parts in this bullshit. It only makes news because they got caught. Them hoes love what they do! They have a inside pimp that's all, he guiding them making sure they safe in the process. You'll always be mad worrying about shit like that." Monte yelled as if he was speaking politically correct to her

Diamond took a long hard look at the 2 and smiled

"I let you have your moment but you have no idea what you're talking about. You think I would care if it wasn't personal" she asked with a half smile on her face. She stood up and tossed the table they were playing cards on. The 2 looked at her like she was crazy

"Mr. Pro woman and Pro black do you know I was a part of that ring but escaped, while you're laughing. Do you know I was raped by that man they call Beast which happened to be my first time! My innocence was taken! Now I couldn't imagine anyone ever touching me again, but it's ok because it happens right? Its normal and we girls enjoy it right. Did you know that same man also killed my mother, but not before impregnating her with me" she cried as she broke down to her knees. P-funk and Monte stood in shock taking in all the information Diamond gave. Monte gave P-Funk a shoulder bump advising him to console her. P-Funk walked over to her kneeled down and hugged her whispering "I'm sorry"

"I don't need your sorry! She said getting back up. Don't feel sorry for me I'm here right now to tell the story! I'm crying because I'm angry not hurt that's the difference. Monte you asked where I came from and why I'm here I WANT FUCKING REVENGE and I know you guys can help me!

"You already know I'm in! Ya story got me boiling inside now this nigga got to go" P-funk replied

"And you Monte?"

"Baby girl what's your plan, you want to actually kill him have you ever killed somebody" Monte asked

"Chill you thinking too far ahead, let the youngin speak bro" P-Funk said

"2" she replied

"2 what" P-Funk responded confused

"He asked have I ever killed anyone. Yes 2 people for reasons like just this one."

"Wait you killed two people. I don't believe that shit. You're what 96 lbs. maybe" Monte said

"What's my weight or sizes have to do with anything? A gun weighs how much and has killed how many people? Exactly! I have a plan in motion, so I will do this with or without you. My original home plan didn't go as plan so when I met P-Funk I utilized the open arms to ensure I had a somewhat of safe a cozy place to lay my head until I was ready to put my plan in motion"

"So, what's your plan?" they asked

"Well I have a friend whose very tech savvy. I paid him to find and keep tabs on Beast. Come to find out he now manages a strip club in Pittsburgh called Sugaa's, I'm sure it's a way to promote girls and sell his drugs. All I really needed was a location figure out his routine and catch him slipping. Everybody loves money so him managing the place plus all the shiesty side business he got going on I figure that's where you guys come in. Catch him one night when he's alone adding up the finances and take him for everything penny he got. Make him take you to the bigger stash if you want, just make sure he stays alive for me. I want him to see me realize and acknowledge who I am before I blow his head off sound like a plan" she said

"Damn! I would hate to get on your bad side. Your little ass came up with all that on your own! You are going be a dangerous woman when you get older. I'm in"

"Yeah me too, Monte agreed"

"Great this probably won't happen for a few weeks from now so that everything's in line. I was waiting to fill you in because I still have a lot of information to collect and make a few more dollars before I can put this plan into motion"

"What you mean dollars? What you working? Is that where you are going every Sunday?" P-funk asked

"Yea something like that" she replied picking up the table

"Man, I'm drunk I'm going the fuck to bed, we'll talk about this shit tomorrow see if you still feel the same" Funk said going up the steps

"This aint no game I'm dead ass" Diamond said emotionally

"No doubt youngin catch you in the a.m. and quit cussing" he yelled back before disappearing into his room

"Alright, well I'm out too but if you serious and sure about this we are going get that nigga alright" Monte said extending his arm for a hug. Diamond reached her arms out to embrace him then responded "alright."

The next day Diamond was up and out the door early. It was Sunday morning and she wanted to make both services at Macedonia. Since she explained her plan to P-funk and Monte she felt like it was time to make some moves to make her plan go a little quicker than expected. She entered the church in her Sunday's best. From going to several services she learned how a lot of the females there dressed so she went out and found similar outfits to blend in just as well as the other ladies did. She had on black and white stripe pants with a red top w/ a long black cardigan and a red cloche hat. She looked like she could've been one of pastor daughters.

This time she sat to the left of the church in the middle of the section where most of the older folks sat not a lot but enough to ensure the plate would come over to that side. She realized the plate usually gets to that side of the church last and its usually filled with the big bucks and this time she planned on taking majority of it. Diamond sat patiently as the pastor gave his Sermon.

"It's always easier to go with what's wrong, that's how the devil works and he works on us easy and well. We've all had those moments of temptation and it could be because of numerous things! The number one thing this here devil strives at getting us with is Revenge. He now had Diamonds full attention. *And yes, revenge feels good real good depending on what it is that you're revenging, but*

that feeling deep inside of you that's pain Amen that's hurt which mean you don't have the control you think you do. You're revenging only further goes to show you don't have that control you think you do Amen. And once you get that revenge although you may be satisfied you still lost. Can I get an Amen? You're still lost because all the collusion and secrets you kept held back or even discussed put whomever you're plotting against in control. You've made them important you've made them "a subject" so who really won. Can I get an Amen"?

"Amen" the church sang. Diamond hated sitting in on the sermons because it's always seemed like the pastor knew everything about every move she was thinking of making or about to do and then the rest of the day she feels guilty. She regained focused and looked around the church and spotted Tauti sitting a few rows in front of her sitting next to Tory. The nerve of her fake ass she thought, she pulled out a piece of paper and wrote {keep a close eye on Tauti she's trying to sleep with the pastor}. She planned to leave it in the pulpit before she left the church. The collection plate went around the usual scheduled time. She opened her big purse and placed it on the floor in between her feet which gave her enough room to just drop the money right into it as she's been. Once the plate got to her row, she scanned it trying to get a fill for how much was in there. She looked around to make sure no one was watching. Once the close was clear she pulled 15 dollars from her pocket placed it slowly in the plate and before passing to the elderly man a few inches away she pushed majority of the money on top of the plate forward landing perfectly in her purse below her and passed the plate on smiling. When she looked up, she noticed the pastor watching her. Not sure if he seen her or not but she continued to smile and clap her hands to the choir's hymns. She decided not to stay for the second service nervous that Pastor Johnson caught her. When the service ended, she blended with the crowd and headed for the front door.

"Why are you still in my city you're not welcome here" Tauti said walking up behind her. Diamond turned around and laughed

"Why are you even talking to me? Why are you even here to wreck their home more than you already are"?

"You shut your damn mouth little girl! Oh, forgive me lord you got me cursing in the church"

"You walked up on me I don't owe you or your family anything and I'm long gone out your hair so I would advise you stay out my way lady before I do something to ruin your life in this town" Diamond said with a serious threatening face

"Ladies, it's always good to see welcoming faces of the church. Did you enjoy today's sermon" Pastor Johnson said. Diamonds eyes got big

"Oh yes pastor what a great word you shared today" Tauti replied in a fake voice

"And you Diamond"

"Oh yes pastor great word" she replied nervously

"Well that's great to hear, Diamond can I have a word with you in my office please?"

"Umm sure I guess, she said grabbing her bag tight and following the pastor" This was it she thought she's caught and going to jail. The 2 reached his office "take a seat please" he gestured, Diamond did as he instructed.

"So how are you" he asked

"Uh I'm good sir is something wrong?"

"Should something be wrong? You're good well that's good you look good too. Almost like real member of this church, he said turning on the monitor. But that's not the case right?" Pastor Johnson replayed 6 different tapes from the security cameras of Diamond stealing from the collection plates. Diamonds heart was in her toes at that moment. The pastor didn't have any emotion on his face he didn't look angry or concerned nothing he just watched. After the last tape ended he stopped the tape and just looked at her; she looked like she saw a ghost. "Now I would ask you to explain but the tapes are self-explanatory. I would ask why but for any person to steal from a church steal from god has to be a pretty good reason."

"Sir just call the cops" she said with her head down

"Diamond, look at me because you're not listening. Do I look upset? Do I look like I want to call any cops?"

"Uh, no but I stole from you so why wouldn't you"

"You know what I got from you the first time I met you? Hurt, pain, anger, and bitterness all from that fake smile and short friendship you and my daughter shared. I am going to be frank with you because I don't know how to be any other way. You can't bullshit a bull shitter. Diamond looked up at him in shock. Yes, I curse at times I'm human so are you and there's nothing wrong with all those things that I read about you after 5 minutes of meeting you. The problem is what you are doing to fix it besides stealing from us."

"I'm on my own I don't have family this is the only way I can...."

"Stop, he interrupted opening his drawer. He pulled out an envelope and handed it to her. Open it!" She looked at him confused but did as he said. The envelope was filled with a large lump sum of cash.

"What! But"

"That's 15 thousand dollars, and I want you to have it"

"But why, she asked as her eyes filled with tears"

"I don't know what you got going on in your life and don't want to know. What I do want you to know is God always find a way if you believe and let go of that hurt! That releases so many negative things about you and teaches you to embrace the good in you. There's a phrase my father taught me coming up and I live by this {It not always about where you've been but where you're going} whatever or whomever hurt you whatever is keeping you from being the best you are in control, gain that control back you deserve it. You still have so time to become the best version of yourself you understand me. That sermon was especially for you I just hope you take heed you don't have to remain a victim" Diamond sat speechless with tears rolling down her face

"Thank, thank you "she stuttered

"You're welcome! Take the money whatever you need to buy or have now you have it. Whatever you're going through you can beat it whatever this is trust me. Now take that and go hopefully I'll still see you every once in awhile and not because I caught you stealing" he joked

"No I promise I won't steal ever again and thank you so much" she said leaving his office. She walked through the church bowled over as so many thoughts ran through her mind. She rushed out the church quick as assuming everyone was watching her. Finally reaching outside she exhaled

"What was that about" Tyrek said scaring Diamond

"What the hell you scared me half to death" she replied

"What were you in my dad's office for?"

"We were just talking, he wanted to know why me, and you sister aren't friends anymore and that she seemed sad not having me around, she lied. w\Why you are jumping out like spider man"

"I seen you earlier and was about to speak than I seen you walking in my dad's office I thought something was wrong"

"Nope everything is all good. I was going to call you. I need that info now all of it and I mean from A-Z"

"Ok no problem, I pretty much got all his steady moves noted. I can get you the full lay out later today. Want to meet up somewhere?"

"Why don't you stop by P-Funk I don't think it will be an issue"

"Diamond what I tell you about him he's bad news and I don't want any affiliation with that fucking psycho"

"Fine I'll leave it at that what's best for you? Meet me at the McDonald on 41st at 630 is that easy for you to get to if not I can pick you up maybe around the corner or something but I'm not coming to his crib."

"That works pick me up around 630 at Woodbridge Park"

"Ok cool I'll see you then" he said going back into the church for the second service

Diamond waited on the swings for Tyrek to pick her up it was 640 and he was officially late. She picked up her phone to call him but his car pulled up in front of her. "Damn I been sitting here forever"

"Quit lying and get your little butt in the car so I can get out of here" he responded. They drove to the McDonalds on 41st as planned. Tyrek ordered food first than sat in the booth with her.

"Such a romantic date" she joked

"Shut up" he said pulling out his laptop

"Ok so as I told you he was the manager of Sugaa's right well he is now indeed co-owner. He bought in with the owner and remodeled the whole establishment which now has the foot traffic of 85 percent of the city. Big difference from the 45 percent they previously had before he took parts so he's doing well for himself. He got one main female in the club. She distributes the cocaine to all the dancers and that's how it gets around the club. I did my calculations from after I tapped in to his business phone and heard a few conversations. It looks like he's currently grossing 20,000 between Thursdays and Sunday night of every week which is huge especially since this is only his side work. The club alone makes a killing too! This is the number 1 strip club in Pittsburgh right now. He does his collects every Sunday night and goes out the back door down the steps where he parks his car to avoid getting robbed. Found that out from my tap into the security system. Yes, I know I'm bad, he joked. He stays in Bellevue north of Pittsburgh. Out the way quiet but still close enough to not have to drive far to get back to the city. He lives alone but he has two other places he goes quite often I think one of them may be his grandmother it's an older lady and one is maybe a baby momma her name is Mercedes."

"How old are her kids"

"From what I got they're older not new babies couldn't get an age though"

"Mercedes! Do you have a last name?"

"Yup it looks like Mercedes Waters" he replied Diamonds eyes grew big

"Are you sure the kids are his?" she asked in disbelief

"Yeah pretty sure, apparently when he decided not to go back to Youngstown he stayed down in Pittsburgh for a few and they reconnected... I have a paternity test on file for them if you want to see. Apparently he didn't think they were his either"

"No its fine, keep going"

"Ok what did I miss? Your whole attitude changed what did I say wrong?" Diamond just looked at him unsure of what to say. Is that why her aunt Mercedes hated her she thought to herself. Did her aunt know all along about Beast? So many thoughts rushed past her mind

"Earth to Diamond, hello, he said breaking her thoughts should I continue"

"Yeah sorry continue" she said fully focused again

"Ok so depending on what you're planning to do with this information and I'm just throwing out a wild thought but the fact that this guy probably has loads of money and live in a fairly all white neighborhood if you for instance wanted to rob him hence you linked up with P-Funk the best time to do so would be on a Sunday night but not at the club go to his house actually get in his house and wait on him there. He has a safe underneath his bed in his guest room built into the floor. Ask me how I know that, he said showing her the camera view of his house. Boom! He laughed out loud. There is probably over 900 thousand dollars in there and at least 7 keys of the purest cocaine. He's been dealing with a Puerto Rican or Mexican can't really tell but it looks like these guys handle nothing but the best. Now on the other hand hence again you linked up with P-Funk if you planned on killing him, on the 3rd and 22nd of every month he goes to the West End overlook at 10 pm and its completely dark and he's always alone. He goes to the 3rd bench haves a seat, smoke a full stogie cigar alone and just watch the city view. Honestly since I've been watching him all these weeks no offense because you didn't tell me too much behind this information you needed my thoughts, he seems like a pretty stand up guys besides the selling drugs and being a womanizer.

Diamond looked at him in disgust "Yeah looks can be deceiving so don't speak on what you don't know ok. She said angrily. Thank you for that information you are good at what you do. Here's the rest of the money I owe you and I am now officially out of your hair."

"Well thank you and you weren't a problem I grew quite fond of your little ass even though you sided with Big Meech," he joked

"He's really not that bad. I think I made him somewhat of a softy actually"

"Yeah ok don't put your guard down I'm telling you" Tyrek reminded her again

"Whatever how can you get all this information to me and off that computer? I need addresses to all the places names times everything"

"That's no problem; here you go he said handing her a flash drive. Everything we just went over is on that drive recordings, times, places, names everything. So, if you don't mind me asking what do you plan to do with it?" He asked biting his burger Diamond sat and thought about the question long and hard

"Well in case anyone has forgotten about me which it seems as if they may have I plan to reintroduce myself"

CHAPTER 15 (Do unto others as you would have them do unto you) Actions don't change so results remain the same and Karma comes fast like a boomerang {**REPRISAL**}

"Who is it?" Diamond yelled skipping down the steps to answer the knocks at the door. No one responded but she could hear a woman's cry's one the other end. Who is it! She yelled again.

"It's Diamond" the woman responded. Diamond opened the door to the crying woman who looked as if she had been beaten badly. She had a black ring around her right eye and blood running from her mouth. Her shirt was ripped and she wasn't wearing any shoes.

"You're the naked lady. Are you okay? Come in" Diamond said

"Yea the naked lady she said cracking a half smile as she limped in the house. You're Diamond right I didn't forget. Is Funk here?"

"No, he hasn't been home since last night, but Monte just left, he said he should be home in a few hours he was handling something. Can I get you something or would you like to use a bathroom?"

"Yes, please I know I probably look hideous. I'm going to grab a shirt out of Funks room too okay" she said walking up the steps. Diamond ran pass her blocking her at the fourth step, "sorry but you're going to have to use the downstairs bathroom and I can grab you a shirt from upstairs"

"What's the problem I've been in his room plenty times"

"Yeah well without him here I can't allow that I'm sure you understand" Diamond said with a fake smile on her face. Big Diamond turned around while Little Diamond followed her back down the steps. She walked into the bathroom and ran the water not taking her eyes off the image of herself she seen in the mirror.

"Look at my face" she cried

"I'll go grab you a wash cloth and t shirt okay" Diamond yelled from the hallway as she ran up the steps. She ruffled through the drawers trying to find a t-shirt for her then got her a wash cloth and towel. Running back down the steps P-Funk came through the door.

"What's up shawty, what wrong why you looking like that?"

"Nothing it's just your friend is here and beaten up pretty bad. I grabbed her clean shirt out your room and wash cloth to clean up."

"My friend who" he said looking around. Diamond limped out the bathroom and began to cry. "Damn Diamond what the fuck happened to you?"

"That nigga Bonez" she responded

"You still fuck with that slob ass nigga!" He yelled helping her to the couch

"No, I'm not; I got booked to do a party in Prince George County. Even though they blood you heard Lil Rock came home? Well Que offered me 5 thousand just to dance for 2 hours; I could use that money, so I said ok. 40 minutes in Bonez drunken ass dragged me out the room naked by my hair she cried. He kept punching and kicking me screaming fuck that protection order bitch and no one would do anything they just turned their heads and let him beat my ass."

"All of them niggaz is bitches to just sit back and watch that shit happen" he yelled angrily

"I got in the car and ran with the little stuff I could grab. I'm calling the cops on his ass he's going to jail" she cried pulling out her phone

"Cops hell no we don't do that shit over this way, Ill handle it" he said pulling out his gun

"Hold up what you fitting to do" Big Diamond asked nervously

"Listen, the nigga don't give a fuck about that piece of paper. You can't even make decent bread because you don't know where he might show up. He's not going leave you alone! So you just are going sit around waiting for the nigga to kill you?" Little Diamond sat on the other couch and just watched the hurt and sadness in her eyes while she talked thinking after all that he's done she still wants to spear his life. Why don't I have that forgiveness in me she thought? She thought about the pastor's words and the money she had tucked away in her bedroom. So many signs telling her to just let it go, forgive those so she can begin to heal.

"So, what you want to happen" P-Funk said interrupting her thoughts

"He got to go" Little Diamond replied. P-Funk and Big Diamond looked up at her "Period you know what time it is" P-Funk agreed picking up his phone. He called Monte and instructed him to find out where Bonez was and to call him when he knew he was by himself. Monte called back in no more than 20 minutes

"Yo, yeah that nigga over at the pool hall solo and wavy off that dirty sprite. I got eyes in there right now on him, said he been in there awhile so he probably going be leaving soon."
"Bet! Meet me over there in 15 this nigga crossroads FAM"
"Bet 100" Monte said before hanging up

"I'll be back stay her until I get back hear me." She nodded with approval and he left. Diamond sat staring at her while she kept her head down with the cold wash cloth on her face.

"I still think you look pretty Tonya" Diamond said trying to break the awkward silence

Big Diamond looked up and smiled "You remember my name"

"Well it was sort of easy since we both answer to Diamond. That could get confusing and you said it's your dance name. You're not dancing now so Tonya it is ok"

Tonya nodded in satisfaction. We got some pizza if you're hungry she said pointing into the kitchen. Come on let me show you."

P-Funk pulled up to Set Em Up pool hall off 495 and parked 2 rows behind Bonez red Q45 and sat with his lights out. Monte tapped on the passenger window and hopped inside.

"So, what's this about? Why we got beef with Bonez?"
"That nigga is still wilding out. Diamond stopped passed all fucked up bloody and shit. She told me she was just trying to make a couple dollars from B Gang and his shaky ass snapped on her fucked her up. She got papers on this nigga and everything he won't stay away. She can't shop can't really go out she is living in a jail trying to avoid this nigga. I got too much love for her to let her go out like that. Besides I don't like this bitch ass nigga anyway.

"You always had a soft spot for Diamond nigga, Monte joked. I'm behind you but you do know this is going to start some controversy with the bloods, right?"

"Nigga there's already controversy with them bitches anyway so be it" he said cocking his pistol

"Alright how you want to do it"

"I'm about to see if his sloppy ass left his door unlock if not I'm going just rock him to sleep when he walks out the spot fuck it" he said putting on his mask

"No doubt I'm parked right there, he said pointing. When you're done hop in my shit it's unmarked. Ill dump it afterwards and come grab your car tomorrow."

"Bet" Monte hopped out the car and walked back to his car. P-Funk crept out the car and ducked low to the red Q45 checking all doors to see if any were unlocked. Bingo he thought, opening the back-passenger door and getting into the car. He kneeled down on the back seat texted Monte {I'm in keep your eyes open and let me know when he come out} Monte Quickly responded {Headed your way 20 seconds}. P-Funk inched up to see if he could see him coming and there Bonez was stumbling through the parking lot trying to find his keys. He pushed the unlock button and stopped next o the car. He opened the door but didn't get in; P-Funk looked confused but heard what sounded like piss. He inched up again and noticed Bonez was pissing outside the car. Bonez turned to get in the car BOOM BOOM BOOM three-gun shots went off hitting Bonez in the chest causing him to fall into the car landing in the driver seat now laying face to face with where P-Funk was laying. His phone lit up {get the fuck out of there now} in text from Monte. P-Funk jumped out the backseat and ran back to his car looking around, but no one was insight. He started his car and pulled off.

"What the fuck happened nigga I told you I had it" P-Funk yelled into the phone at Monte

"Nigga that wasn't me I was sitting in my car watching the whole thing!

"Well who was it then?"

"I couldn't tell dude had on a hoodie and came out of nowhere. Bonez start pissing turned to get in the car and dude appeared. He had to have said something to him because he turned back around, and dude shot him then ran. Is he dead?"

"It looked like it, but he made eye contact with me so if he aint we really going have problems"

"Who the fuck was that though shits crazy, just go to the crib I'll keep my ears and eyes open and let you know what's up" Monte said

"No doubt get at me: he said hanging up

P-Funk entered the house to see Tonya on the floor watching TV sitting in between Diamonds legs as she brushed her hair. Tonya jumped up when she noticed him walking in

"How did everything go?" she asked nervously

"Man, I'm so confused I do…"

"Wait should she go upstairs first" Tonya asked

"No shawty more thorough than you think she cool. So, I had the drop and location got over there laid on him and before I could do anything somebody else got to him first."

"What you mean" she asked confused

"Just like I said I was laying in his backseat he opened the door to get in and somebody shot him 3 times. We made eye contact as he was slumped over the seat, but he must have had other beef because somebody had the same idea as me."

"So is he dead or what?"

"It sure as hell looked like it! Guess we soon shall see. He said grabbing a piece of pizza. What you two into though I aint worried about shit.

"Nothing just doing girl stuff thought I'd take advantage since there are never any girls around here." Diamond said

"Oh you are trying to flex! So what you saying, I aint no fun. Dime who taught you how to clean guns blind folded? She aint teach you that" he joked

Funks phone rang "Hello"

"Nigga turn on channel 10" Monte yelled from the other end. Funk turned on the news which flashed a video capturing his silhouette as he ran from the red Q45 during the shooting of Jovan Miller aka Bonez who is in critical condition after 3 gunshot wounds to the back. If anyone has any information or can identify who this male is, please contact the Virginia P.D

"What the fuck" he said to himself

"I'm sorry to say but this aint looking good on either end! We got the jakes on one end and now the bloods on the other. Anybody that knows you can tell that's you." Monte said

"Nigga don't you think I know that" he snapped, I got to get up out of here till I figure out what's going on"

"Well I have a suggestion, Diamond interrupted. I was able to get all the information I needed about that situation we talked about the other day. I got money saved up enough to be good now and you need somewhere to go so let's go to Pittsburgh!"

"Pittsburgh? You still stuck on old dude" Diamond looked at him with a serious face. "Oh, you thought I was going forget, I plan to do this, but I can really use your help. From what I was told he got over 500k in his house and I happen to have the address" she said

"Man Listen I don't know about you but that sound like the move, either way we got to get the fuck out of dodge fam" Monte replied

"Listen meet me at The Silk Mill my peoples run the spot I'll let you know the room number. Ditch your car I'll do the same see you in a minute" P-Funk said hanging up. Diamond me and lil shawty got to cut babe that niggaz basically dead them bullets hit crazy, so you cool now you can get back to business as usual. Keep your mouth shut and you should be cool.

"That aint for sure though. We can't trust that! I want to go with yall" Tonya said

"No can do… this is some hot shit stay out the way"

"Well technically she might be helpful Diamond interrupted he is co-owner of a strip club called Sugaa's. I think she could help in a big way" P-Funk looked at her as his wheels start turning. "You always so quick on your toes have been here before" he joked

"Alright gather up yall shit we out then" he said Diamond grabbed a few things and the laptop and the 3 left the house. They pulled up to the Silk Miles Motel where 2 officers sitting in the lobby eating donuts. P-Funk advised Tonya to go into the hotel and book the room handing her the money while they waited in the car.
"So where did you get the drop on dude from?" he asked Diamond while they waited

"I got my connections" she joked

"Oh, so your big time now, you know this shit you want to happen is real shit right big boy big girl shit"

"Yup and I'm ready to take that niggaz head off" Diamond responded

"Quit cussing" they both laughed Tonya walked out with the key to the room. Advised him it was a suite and she got it for 2 days just in case. P-Funk sent Monte the room information and headed up to the room from the side entrance avoiding any cameras and police in lobby.

"Aright youngin so your source told you straight facts that he had that much money in the crib or he said he thinks?"

"I saw it myself; he gave me a video that he had. He hacked into his house cameras I have everything on file. Do you want to wait for Monte or should I show u now" she asked?

"Show me the safe, you can go over the plan later I need to see that this is worth it" Diamond pulled out her laptop and inserted the flash drive. When she opened the file that read Open Me all the save files and recording popped up on the screen at once. She navigated through the files and pictures and seen the familiar video of Beast at his house right before placing money into the safe.

"Pay attention" she said slowing down the video. P-Funk watched as Beast went into his guest bedroom lifted the bed and pulled up the floor that lead to the hidden safe, opening it and placing 3 bricks of money into the safe.

"Fucking Jackpot" he jumped up happily Lil mama you just made my day. We about to bleed that nigga dry" He said dancing around in excitement. Diamond didn't care about the money she wanted him dead and that's all she cared about.

"So how do I help" Tonya asked

"Chill let's wait for Monte so she don't have to repeat herself he should be here any minute." He interrupted

"Well you'll be doing what you do oh so well, showing off your pretty face and body. I want you to go in the club like you're looking for a job try to get a feel for the place. Better yet try to get close to him. I figure if we could get in easy by just following you somewhere that may be easier. If not of course there are always other options." Diamond continued ignoring P-Funk. He picked up his phone to call Monte to see where he was and got no answer. "Hurry up nigga! We all here 3rd floor room 423" he said leaving the message. Go head you might as well start I don't know where this nigga is."

Diamond pulled up all the video footage she had carefully explaining exactly what was what and who was who. "That's Beast in the yellow and his partner in the Purple that's standing next to the bartender. Those two are the big guys the money makers but dude in the yellow is who I want no one touches him but me. The person who gave me all the info been tracking him for about 3 months and he has a steady pattern, so it shouldn't be hard to get to him one way or another. I figure you guys go in get dressed up get a good inside look of the place even closer look at him and go from there. Tonya can try to get close to him or his partner." Diamond was interrupted my banging on the door. P-Funk pulled his gun out "WHO IS IT" no one responded on the other end. He peeked out the door spotting Monte bleeding as he slid down the wall trying to hold himself up. P-Funk opened the door and dragged him inside. He was holding a bag full of guns with almost 5 thousand in it.

"Fuck! Who did this shit! What happened, he said in a panic looking for the wound he was bleeding from" Monte had a gunshot wound to the stomach. He laid him down on the floor. Tonya pulled Diamond into the bathroom, so she wouldn't see what was happening.

"Cuz look at me what happen" P-Funk kept repeating

"B gang B gang, he repeated in between gasps"

"B gang did this to you them bitch ass niggaz man don't talk. I'm going get you to a hospital ok pull through FAM, I got to just drop you in the front you know I can't go in" Monte shook his head no. "I robbed them niggaz he mumbled, they were talking crazy said they coming for you for that Bonez shit so I robbed them niggaz and took everything"

"If I don't take you, you're going die! The bullet went through your stomach bro" Sirens rang as cops approached the hotel. Diamond ran to the window. "The cops!" she yelled P-Funk tried to pick Monte up off the ground he screamed in agony.

"Just go leave me here take the bag handle the bizz. I'll be aright"

"I'm not leaving you here" P-Funk yelled as he tried to pick him back up

"Ahhh Monte screamed I can't be moved this shit is going kill me quicker than I'm already dying, at least they can get me to the hospital. Just go hurry up" he pled. P-Funk took one last look at him hugged him and ran out the room as the girls followed. The car was parked on the same side the cop cars were lined up as they swarmed into the building. The 3 walked out the rear entrance and kept walking until they were off the hotel property and on the main road. Tonya requested an Uber under her sister's account to take them back to her apartment where her car was. P-Funk didn't waste any time once they got there. The three hopped in her car and hit 495 towards Breeze wood. Everyone rode in silence as he checked his phone for messages or posts on Monte's condition but nobody knew anything. He had to focus on getting that money and getting far away from VA for good.

6 hours later the 3 finally reached Monroeville, Pa small town on the outskirts of Pittsburgh. They stopped in Panera Bread in the Miracle Mile mall grabbed something to eat as they went over their plan.

"Aright we are going grab a telly Diamond you are going stay there while me and Diamond go check the club out"

"Call me Tonya" she replied it's just less confusing calling out Diamond and we both answer but ok we are going check out the spot I'm listening"

"Yea we just doing research for a few days make sure none of his moves switch up from what you showed us so far and go from there"

"Why can't I come, I can wait in the car"

"Can't risk no one seeing you especially if they remember your face"

"It's not they it's just him and I'm sure he will remember my face"

"Don't worry you going get your time to shine I promise you" Diamond pouted at the thought of being treated like a little girl

"So, when are we doing this tonight?" Tonya asked

"Yeah it's probably going be the next 3 nights just to make sure we got the move and give you time to work your magic on him" P-Funk phone rang

"Who this, he answered"

"Looks like you got yourself in quite a spin my man. I thought we had an understanding! You stay on your side and I'll stay on mine. Some leader you are, your mans is dead all because you can't respect the rules and the way they played"

"Fuck is this"

"Red! Yeah wake the fuck up nigga, see cause now we really got a problem"

"I'm around catch me before I catch you bitch ass nigga" P-Funk said before hanging up. He slammed his fist on the table "Fuck, fuck he yelled"

"What's wrong" Diamond yelled frightened.

"Monte is dead and I'm sure there's a hit on my head so I guess I'm next that was Red"

"I'm so sorry I know this is all my fault"

"It's cool man don't nobody know where I'm at. Ill handle that bullshit later let's get this money.

Chapter 16 (What lies beneath a broken soul yet plays side by side a scorned heart) The angry faded shadow that's hidden in the dark, an unseen figure lurks waiting for that dangerous flame to be sparked {**WRATHFUL**}

"Don't act new to this shit perk them titties up! You want to get the whole club's attention when you walk in" P-Funk said helping Tonya with her shirt. The 2 sat outside the club watching the foot traffic that went in and out before they walked in.

"Bingo that's your man's right there" he said pointing his gun finger at Beast as he walked by.

Tonya walked in ahead of P-Funk so it wouldn't seem like the two were together. Her caramel skin glistened of the dim light reflecting from the stage. She walked to an empty round table in the middle of the floor and sat down close to the stage. P-Funk walked in and sat at the bar.

"Let me get a Henny & Coke" he said looking around the club through the mirror behind the bar. Tonya watched the 3 girls on stage thrusting and grinding on each other however she was not enthused. The crowd looked bored watching the interaction between the girls and no money was being thrown. After getting an idea of the crowd she walked up to the stage and threw 50 ones in the air.

"I want to see some asses shake and some pussy's pop hit the pole mama" she yelled out waking the crowd up. The Puerto Rican dancer stood up and seductively walked over to the pole. She stood at about 6ft with the 6-inch heels she had on. Her skin was like butter and her hair fell down a little past her ass. She wrapped her long legs around the pole and inched her way all the way to the top. She gripped her legs tight and firm careful to balance and threw herself back exposing her succulent D cup breast and pink nipples. P-Funk sipped his drink as he watched Tonya work. Tonya yelled in approval as she twirled around the top of the pole. The crowd got involved cheering her on as well. Tonya yelled louder as she slid down the pole and dropped into a split. Tonya was dressed in a See-through netted dress with neon pink bra and panty set with 6-inch clear high heels. The dancers on stage try to impress her assuming she was a dancer from another city. Tonya continued to throw money and all the girls gravitated towards her getting majority of the club's attention including Beast who was watching through the security cameras. P-Funk watched with approval.

    One of the girls pulled her up on stage and cheered her on to dance. She noticed P-Funk now sitting in the second row back directly in front of her nodding her to go with it. Tonya began to slowly wind in the middle of the stage now having the entire club's attention. Her look was so exotic there was no way you could look away. One of the girls on stage stood in shock as she watched her. Tonya slid down to the floor inching into a split while clapping her ass on the floor. Beast came out to the floor and advised the bartender to bring him a bottle of Cîroc as he watched her dance. The bait was working; P-Funk got up and moved to the back of the club out of sight. Everyone clapped and cheered her on as the song ended, she smiled and walked off the stage and was approached by the bartender.

"Hi Miss" she paused

"Oh Diamond my name is Diamond"

"Miss Diamond, the gentleman in the VIP would like you to join him" Diamond looked up to VIP to see who she was referring to and notice Beast directing her to the V.I.P section. She proceeded to walk in his direction.

"So, you got it like that you just send for what you want" she said sitting down next him"

"I wouldn't say all that, but I'm known to get what I want usually"

"Is that right? So, what is it that you want?" she said flirtatiously

"Well first I want to know who you are and where the hell you been? Dancing like that, shit looking like that, I know this aint your first time. You looking for a job baby?"

"You're cute but do I look like I need a job" she said flashing her body? Beast eyes got lost in the creases of her thighs as she spread her legs.

"Damn baby, you got to chill before I eat that pussy right here, you want a drink?" he said pouring 2 glasses. P-Funk walked out the club to call Diamond and fill her in on how smoothly everything was going.

"Hello, she answered whispering

"This shit is going be like taking candy shawty she in there sucking his ass up whole" He said laughing in excitement.

"Really that's great" she whispered

"Why you are whispering what's wrong" he asked sounding worried"

"Oh, nothing I just stepped out for some fresh air and to check up on some stuff"

"Diamond what the fuck! This aint your city you can't just be out here by yourself anything can happen to you"

"I didn't know you cared, she joked still whispering it's all good I'm cool just wanted to get some air on my way back now." she lied

"Aright we'll be there in a minute; I'm thinking we can get this over with ASAP if you know what I mean"

"Too soon and I told you what I want we had a deal,"

"But Diamond he's right there I can handle everything for you. You can keep your hands clean"

"No, I want to do it myself don't ruin this for me" she pled

"Ok relax its all you. We about to get up out here so see you in a minute" he said hanging up the phone and going back into to the club.

Diamond stood across the street from the Bedford Dwelling housing glaring through the open window. She watched as her aunt Mercedes combed her hair in front of her vanity with no worry in the world. The portraits of Beast and the twins were decorated all over the mantle of the living room along with a portrait of just Mercedes and Beast which looked like one big happy family. The site of it made Diamonds skin boil! She wanted to knock on her door but didn't want to make any un-rational moves without a plan. So instead she just watched her reminding herself that her days were numbered.

"Can I help you?" an elder lady asked opening her door to the house Diamond was standing in front of.

"Oh no ma'am just waiting on my ride" she replied with a smile

"Well you're more than welcome to stand in my door way to get you out the rain honey" she generously offered

"Thank you miss but it shows he's a minute away" she said smiling "Ok" the lady waved closing her door behind her. Mercedes walked out her front door opened her umbrella and began to walk down Bedford Ave heading towards town. Diamond followed her trying to be as discrete as possible. Mercedes walked about 3 blocks without looking back but knew there was someone following her. Diamond kept her distance but stayed on her heels curious as to where she was walking at that time of night alone. Mercedes turned the corner out of Diamonds sight; she sped up to catch her. Mercedes grabbed her slamming her into the wall.

"Why the fuck is you following me she yelled with her fist balled. She realized it was Diamond. Diamond what the fuck are you doing here and why are you following me! Are you alone?"

"Yes, I didn't have anywhere else to go. So, I searched for your address online hoping I can maybe stay with you awhile." She lied

"I told you before I can't do anything for you. I got my own kids to worry about and a man. I don't have time for you and your bullshit so try someone else"

"But I don't have anyone else and I never gave you any bullshit not ever" she cried

"NOT MY PROBLEM and don't follow me" Mercedes said walking away

"But I'm your family she yelled out" Mercedes kept walking ignoring her.

P-Funk signals Tonya to wrap and he left back out the club. She nodded with approval sitting on his lap while he kissed all over her neck and exposed breast. "I got to go baby" she said interrupting him

"No you don't! Where you going you coming with me right" he said not taking his mouth off her body. "I can't tonight I have business to attend to. You understand right?"

"Damn baby when will I going see you again"

"Real soon promise just be patient ok" she said getting up. Beast watched her walk away completely shell shock by the curves. "Boss Brian's back again he's in the champagne room drunk grabbing all over the girls." One of the dancers said

"Where Big Case or Ray"

"We don't know but he got to go like now. He threw up all over the couch and everything"

"Got damn it man who the fuck let him back in" he yelled getting up. The 2 walked back into the champagne room. Brian was laid out on the couch in his own spit up with his pants half down. Beast tapped him, but he didn't budge. He made one of the girls get a bucket of cold water. He poured it on him causing him to jump up.

"What the fuck B! You fucking up my establishment again"

"Nah I'm just having some fun I spend money in here I deserve a piece of pussy if I want it" he slurred

"It doesn't work like that man! You got to go and this time you can't come back hear me"

"Nigga shut your bitch ass up; I'll buy this place and become your boss! I'll come back tomorrow and the day after and you niggaz won't do shit. You think you the man now huh you got the power nigga fuck you." he yelled stumbling

"Listen, I'm not going take too much more of your disrespect. Just get your shit and get the fuck out of my establishment" Beast said keeping his composure.

"Boss mans everything cool" Big Case and Ray said entering the room. Ray and Case were the security of the club and several other clubs in Pittsburgh. Both weighed 300 solid muscles 6'5 in height. "Yeah, I'm good, but of course Brian on his bullshit again! Get his ass out of here through the back so he don't shake up the place"

"I'm not going no fucking where" he yelled aggressively. Ray grabbed him up in a bear hug and Case grabbed his legs and they carried him out the back door. P-Funk and Tonya were still in the parking lot casing the perimeter. When she saw Beast she ducked in the front seat so he wouldn't see her as P-Funk drove past them.

"Shit did he see me" she panicked

"No, he wasn't paying you any attention. Whoever those big ass guards were holding was throwing up everywhere. That pretty ass nigga was looking down at his shoes making sure wasn't nothing on them. So what you get out of him?" he said merging on to 376.

"Well we didn't do much talking, "she smiled; P-Funk looked at her with a straight face waiting for her to say something worth listening to.

"Ok well he's into me so that's a good thing. I think we should wait at least 2 days before I show up again. I didn't give him a number or nothing so I know he is going be looking for me it's the perfect plot. Set him up; take his money boom POW done."

"Yeah let's just hope it's that simple" he said pulling up to the hotel. Diamond still wasn't in the room. P-Funk called her cell numerous times with no answer. "Call me back fuck is you at" he yelled to the voicemail. He paced back and forth thinking the worse happened to her. In little time he became extremely over protective of her since she told him about her past and even grew a little small soft spot for her. Coming from nothing and just trying make it, knowing she was out here alone is this dog eat dog world he couldn't allow himself to just let her drown. Diamond walked in the nonchalant with donuts.

"Where the fuck you been! You aint see me calling"

"My phone died Jesus" she responded

"You can't just be out her with dead phones and shit we not in Va. Somebody could've remembered your face and took your little ass" Diamond pulled out a gun

"Do I look like I'm in any position to be took" she said flashing it

"You went in my bag too" he said snatching the gun

"Funk as bad as you want me to be, I'm not a little girl I can handle more than you think so please get your head in the game and fill me in on the progress."

"Ok, Tonya interrupted you two fight like brother and sister. Ok Dime so Beast was in there like you said."

"You say him" she responded with her full attention

"Say him girl I got him wrapped around my finger now, he was all over me. Everything is going as planned.

He probably thinks I'm just some gorgeous gift from god ha-ha nope boom rock a bye baby" she joked

"He touched you?" she asked

"A little but nothing crazy just a little tease, it always works. You'll learn that as you get older. Don't worry though we are going to get his ass for what he did to you"

"Listen, since the bait was planted smoothly in 2 days it's going down. Tonya you going go up in there do your thing and get him to leave the club with you. Me and Diamond going be waiting outside in the parking lot so make sure you exit out onto 9th street. More than likely he is taking you to a hotel if he smart. Once you get up their text me the info. Diamond you are going to stay your little ass in the car until I get to his ass. Tonya, make sure you leave that door unlocked, I'm coming in there and laying his ass down. We are taking his ass to the safe. So you going hop in my car Ill hop in his and we ride out. Once I get the money Diamond I'll let you do your thing and then we out 500 g's richer ya heard" he said smiling and dancing.

Diamond starred out the window in deep thought. She had so many emotions built up sadness anger happiness. P-Funk was the only person she could consider family at this moment. Mercedes looked at her like she was trash and left her in the streets again. How could she be so stupid to think anything changed she thought?

"Funk once we get the money then what happens" she asked

"We get out of sight; I don't see a reason for going back to VA with niggaz trying kill me. My cousin is dead aint shit left for me there so we going to make a new life somewhere else. We will have plenty of ones to do so."

"We?" she repeated

"Yeah we, I mean you got other plans? Where you planning to go" he asked

"No, I just thought since I asked to stay for a little while until I figured out my plan that maybe after the plan was completed, I would go my own way" she timidly said with her head down

"Shawty from the looks of things you stuck with me for a little while. Besides what you going do with all that money by yourself by some dolls, he joked. No but seriously you are welcome to stay with me if you want. I now consider you family youngin" he said sincerely. Diamond smiled from ear to ear and nodded ok.

"Oh, I got a little surprise for your little snooping ass too." He said pulling a silencer out the drawer. Good thing you didn't bust off that gun you would have been caught in 5 minutes. This right here is a silencer and trust me you'll need it." Diamond took the silencer and screwed it into her 40 Cal she took out the bag. "Perfect" she said to herself.

"Diamond do you really think you will be able to go through with it" Tonya asked

"You want to stand back and watch" she answered the look in her eyes meant business and she was ready for it.

"Its 6 o'clock in the fucking morning where have you been? I been calling you all night" Mercedes screamed sitting up on the couch waiting

"I had business to handle money don't sleep and you know this" Beast responded

"Ok but why didn't you answer?"
"I was working man damn, why you up this early anyway?" he asked

"I couldn't sleep"
"Awww I had you worried he said kissing her forehead

"Actually no, you had me pissed my niece got me worried"

"Ya niece I aint never heard of no niece!"

"Well that's because there was never anything to hear about her. She popped up at the house looking for a place to stay. I always resented this little girl for so many different reasons, but I feel bad about how I just treated her. She was in the rain by herself I don't know where she came from or where she was going. I heard about some crazy shit that went down in Youngstown so who knows what's going on with her now. I don't know I guess she may have pulled a heart string. Lord knows I was terrible to that girl"

"Well did you get the girls info phone number anything?"

"No I just told her no and walked away"

"Damn that's fucked up! Oh well aint shit you can do about it now" he said

"I know, she said sadly I just can't get Diamonds face out my head"

"Diamond" he repeated

"Yeah that's my nieces name she's Cyn's daughter. I don't think anybody knew about her from the past except Bam's ass. I think that was really her dad but aint nobody wanted to say shit. Beast tensed up. What's wrong with you" she said

"Nothing I got a bad migraine, I think I'm going go to the crib I'm not really sleepy mind as well get some work done" he said putting his coat on

"What but you just got here, I don't want you to leave I been waiting for you all night"

"Baby I'm trying to get all the money I can, so I can relax with my feet up sooner than later. You got to stop trying to get in the way of that or I promise you I'll go ghost again. Enjoy the luxury of this shit and bite your tongue you getting on my nerves with this shit." Beast left the house looking around to see if she was lurking anywhere. He rode around the hill district hoping to spot Diamond walking around, but she was nowhere in sight. He knew that was his daughter despite the terrible thing he did to her. There was no way to make it right but money solved all problems in his eyes. His plan was to give her a few thousand to disappear comfortably and forget about her, there was no way to mend a father and daughter relationship after that. It's been sometime he barely remembered what she looked like but figured it was worth a try.

"Hello" he answered his phone

"Is there another bitch"

"Mercedes don't start this shit man"

"Everything is about you, your money and that club; she cried you barely see the kids anymore. You find reasons to go to your house when you used to always stay here"

"I'm fucking working" he yelled

"I just miss you I miss us, were so distant now. It seems like there's someone else."

"I got a headache I can't deal with this shit right now talk to you later" he said hanging up. He pulled up to the 7/11 on liberty where Stacks was parked.

"What's up nigga heard you was Usher last night love in the club ass nigga. Who was that bad ass bitch"?

"Oh yea, shawty was a thick one right! She from Dc here until next week"

"Did you hit that?"

"Man hell no she ass ran out like Cinderella last

night. I was mad as hell but I'm sure I'm going run into her bad ass again. Shit I was trying hire her, she killed my stage last night had the other hoes tipping her." The 2 laughed

"Yea I'll be by tonight to do balances and deposits. I spoke to Druzy today he told me to tell you what's up"

"Oh yea how is her doing? Did he get that money I sent up there?"

"Yeah he said thanks too. That nigga cool up there living like a boss. You know cant no Pen hold that nigga back"

"I hear that! Well No doubt I'll see you tonight then" he said getting back in his car and pulling off.

"I'm getting antsy I can't wait anymore let's do it tonight" Diamond said cleaning her gun

"Rushing things can ruin things remember that" P-Funk said

"What are we rushing? We got a plan were just sitting ducks and for what. Its Friday night the club will probably be crowded so she won't be the focus. She's still fresh on his mind today is perfect" she explained

"You know what this is your plan so if that's what you want to do then fuck it tonight it's on. Just make sure you ready this aint no field trip. All that anger you got built up inside you. All that hurt use it! This will be your first time seeing this nigga since he hurt you. Don't bitch up handle your business feel me"

"I feel you, tonight's the night"

Chapter 17 (Gravity can instantly become one's strategic life lesson) anything thrown up almost always comes down no holds barred what goes around always come back around {**KARMA**}

Diamond watched as Tonya shaved her body. Tonya enjoyed Diamonds curiosity as she slowly went u and down her thigh with the razor.

"Why you are looking so hard child, you act like you never shaved before." Tonya said not taking her eye off her thighs

"Well I haven't" Diamond replied. Tonya looked at her confused. Diamond was a lot taller and more physically built then most girls her age. She could easily pass for a 17year old if needed.

"There is no way you're comfortable with that wolf bush between your legs girlfriend" Tonya replied. Diamond looked down at her crouch confused as to why the long-tangled hair coming from her vagina never bothered her or even resembled a wolf bush in her eyes.

"Well I have some time before we go to the club, I can teach you! If u want, we both know P-Funk won't have the chance too" she laughed

"Will it hurt" Diamond responded nervously

"Not how I teach! A lot of these young girls don't know that when you shave down there you must go against the grain to avoid bumps and irritation. Most of the time, they sneaking to get a clean cat pass they momma. So it usually ends up bumpy and itchy but I can show you come here and take off your bottoms" she said grabbing a new razor. Diamond stood nervously at the fact that she had to take off her bottoms in front of another person especially Tonya seeing as that her body was way better looking a filled out as a grown woman.

"Well, she stood holding the razor. Diamond walked into the bathroom and began to take off her socks. Honey trust me I've then seen more than enough believe me" she laughed. Diamond never thought she would be taking her clothes off in front of anyone ever again but felt comfortable and intrigued by Tonya. She unbuttoned her pants and slowly pulled them off reveling nothing underneath.

"Girl you are full of surprises, why aint you got on no panties?

"I didn't have any clean ones an aint get around to buying anymore" she responded bashfully

"Well just like I thought you got the case of the wolf, she joked so in your case we are going to use some scissors first ok. It's easier if you just stand up and relax. I would hate to cut your little lips off" Diamond smiled embarrassed. Tonya grabbed as much hair as she could in one grip and cut as close to the skin without touching and repeated the steps 3 times. Diamond looked down when she was finished amazed at the great difference it made.

"Wow" she responded

"Wow, girl I'm only half way done! I'm going to clean it up nice and smooth like a baby. Okay lay down right here" Diamond laid back on the counter of the bathroom while Tonya applied shaving cream to her pure and natural unshaved vagina. Diamond laid back trying to remain as steady as she could but beads of sweat began to appear on her head as the flash backs began to cloud her mind.

"Almost done, Tonya said as Diamond tried to keep her composure. Done!" she yelled she noticed the uncomfortable state Diamond was in.

"Take a look girlfriend." She advised as Diamond stood up looking at her body. For the first time she didn't see that little disgusting girl she dreaded looking at when she got out the shower. She saw a woman, a pretty woman, a glowing woman, a woman who was finally happy.

"I look like you" she said not taking her eyes off herself

"Whoa there calm down, not quite there yet but you are a very gorgeous girl" Tonya said standing behind her looking in the mirror at her body

"You think I'm gorgeous, Diamond turned around

"Of course!" she replied. Diamond placed her hand on Tonya's thigh as she slowly grabbed her robe causing it to drop to the floor.

"Dime do you know what you're doing" Tonya asked as she let Diamond rub on her now exposed vagina"

"No, I don't but I like it" she smiled. Tonya stood and let her continue to see where she wanted to go with it. Diamond knew from how her body was that Tonya's couldn't be too much different. Diamond inserted he finger into Tonya's vagina. Tonya released a soft moan causing Diamond to feel a tingle between her legs she's never felt before. Tonya couldn't fight the feeling anymore, she grabbed her face deeply caressing her tongue with hers. This was Diamonds first kiss and Tonya could feel her body trembling nervously. She placed her hand in the back of her head to push her tongue deeper into her mouth. Although she was nervous, the body fluids that poured down her inner thighs told a different story.

"Yo where yall at" P-Funk screamed as the door slammed behind him. Diamond snapped back into reality grabbing a towel.

"Shhhh its ok just go ahead and get in the shower so we can get dressed and get moving. It's ok you did nothing wrong." Tonya said putting her robe back on. She excited the bathroom while Diamond started the shower.

"Hey boo what's that" Tonya said watching P-Funk lay everything out on the bed"

"Ok so check it! Last time you went up in there solo which was cool. I played the back ground and you did your thing. To some niggaz who think like me you coming back randomly by yourself again might have a nigga wondering like who the fuck sent her right. So...... he said unzipping his garment bag. I figured we go up in there together looking like a bag of money. You do your thing I'm going still play my part stay out your way but make it a little easier by the end of the night when we get that nigga you know no surprising faces cause Ill already be that familiar face feel me. Check out this chain with the matching watch, he bragged I'm about to kill em literally" he joked

"This is nice, Tonya said admiring his things. Diamond exited the bathroom fully dressed but avoided eye contact with Tonya.

"What's this stuff" she asked

"Just my little upgrade for the night you know to play my part, oh and for you. P-Funk said pulling out a bag. Now this right here I felt fit perfectly for the night activities. Usually despite your little orders I planned to just handle business myself but you've shown me you a little rider and you got shit covered. So that little chip on your shoulder I'm going let you take a bite feel me." P-Funk laid out a black hoodie with a matching one shoulder duffle bag and hat that read GetMGrl

"Now this I like! Its big enough to hold all my guns and laptop" she said

"You damn right, that's bad ass right there make a statement, stand your ground we bend but not broken facts"

"I like it, I got some black lipstick for you too" Tonya jumped in

"Listen I'll wear whatever just make sure I get him alone and vulnerable" she said walking over to the window. The view wasn't much but she watched all the cars driving on the turnpike. She seen kids smiling and conversing with their families and couldn't help but wonder why her life could never have just been that easy. Then there's Tonya, as confused as she was she knew she had feel in love with her. At first the feeling that she felt when she seen her beaten and bruised was sadness. After spending time with her the feelings she felt was the love she would have felt for a mother. Now after the tingling feeling from the soft moans that came from Tonya when she touched her she knew it was lust. Did that make her gay she thought?

"Dime you ok I know you aint getting cold feet on me? P-Funk asked looking worried

"Yea I'm fine and no just thinking about life after this"

"Shit beaches, fine eating and lavish life lil mama, you only seen what he may have I'm sure that nigga got more and I'm taking it all, he said cocking back his gun. Don't worry shorty I'm going make sure you straight regardless we all we got now. I know if I go back to VA, I got a fucking ticket on my head. And I aint never feared no man but god but I'm no dummy. If I get taken out by them bitch ass niggaz you back to square one. So, we pushing through and headed somewhere far maybe down South leaving all the bullshit behind feel me"

"That sounds nice" she smiled

The 3 hit the parkway towards downtown Pittsburgh. Diamond sat in the backseat with a blank stare on her face. Tonya watched her in the rear view as she drove wondering what was on her mind. She still remembered the day she first started dancing and how she felt when Candy a much older dancer than her at the time touched her for the first time. She was scared shitless, but she was so gentle with her she didn't think it was a bad thing. She liked it, but that same face Diamond has was the same face she had when she left the club that night. It was a look of shame.

"You ok back there" she said interrupting her own thoughts. Diamond responded yeah without eye contact fully staring out the window.

"Are you sure? you awfully quiet for what's about to go down. You got this lil mama"

Diamond was now fully facing her. "I got this I got different plans though; drop me off at his house! I'll find my own way in and I see you two when you get there."

"Huh! P-Funk turned around that wasn't the plan! You were supposed to lay low in the ride until we come out and we going follow him" he said

"Plans changed! We don't even know if he is going bite the bait this time especially with you there. What if he doesn't even bring her back to his house? Better yet what make you think I want to sit in this back seat for hours just waiting NO I'm not doing it. If he doesn't take the bait guess what he still got to come home! Tonight's the night and I'm not messing this up. So it will be with or without you Period!" she said firmly

"But then what Diamond? Your little ass going take him by yourself" Tonya asked

"I've took more than you think if you know what I mean" she responded in a sassy tone

"I don't like this man, there are cameras codes all types of shit you got to do!"

"Fool I'm the one who told you all that what make you think I don't know. I got it covered TRUST ME! You can't keep treating me like a kid especially since we all in this plan to get rich together. I need to feel like I'm part of the team not getting babysat. Today may end up being one of the most important days of my life believe it or not. So show me some fucking respect" She yelled cocking her gun back. The 3 looked around at each other in silence then all started laughing.

"I feel you shorty I know you can hold you own" P-Funk said

"So, detour then" Tonya said yielding onto Pa-65 towards Bellevue where Beast resided. Tonya pulled up to the rear end of the house that was fenced in with high white fencing. You could see the cameras angled from the back porch.

"This looks too risky why can't you just wait?" P-Funk asked

"I got this she said putting her hood over her head. My phone is on keep me updated" she said creeping out the back door blending in with the nightlight. The two watched as she flung herself over the fence like a little ninja. "Damn!" The two said at the same time.

"You know what I think she's ok Funk I trust her" Tonya said. P-Funk didn't take his eyes off of her as she weaved through the trees in the yard "I think your right let's be out" he said advising her to pull off. Diamond looked back noticing the car driving away. There were cameras to the left and right of her but her little body managed to wedge in between a blind spot she noticed while watching the recording that were given to her. She pulled out her laptop to view the inside of the house. From the view she had it looks like she was outside the kitchen. The keypad for the alarm system sat on the hallway wall directly next to the light switch. Diamond texted Tyrek {Work your magic I'm here}. What P-Funk and Tonya didn't know is that Diamond already had access to get into Beast's house and it was only a text away.

    Diamonds phone lit up {Done Be SAFE} Diamond peeked up and noticed the motion sensors lights were off but the video on the laptop showed they were still on. She smiled and responded: {Pure genius} with a kissy face and proceeded to enter the house. Mr. Money bags, she thought admiring the kitchen." I'm going to have a field day with you" she said to herself pulling gout her guns and plastic gloves.

    Tonya and P-Funk sat in VIP drinking and ordering lap dances trying to get as much attention as possible in the club. He was wearing a full-length Burgundy mink coat with gold plated Ray Bans on that matched Tonya's yellow gold diamond corset leather burgundy skirt barely covering her. She danced to the music drinking out the bottle while P-Funk scoped the club trying to spot Beast who was in the corner watching her every move. "Yeah, he yelled smacking her ass, all eyes on you do your thing" P-Funk said making her aware that she caught Beast eye. Tonya slowly grinded to the music: trying to spot where Beast was sitting but couldn't get a good look due to the bright lighting.

"I don't see him" she said smiling through her concerned face. Beast walked up behind her. "Hello and welcome to Sugaa's I hope you and your husband are comfortable. Is there anything I can get you two? Tonya looked at him confused

"Oh, you think! No, you don't have to be so formal this is my brother" she laughed

"Girl you don't know how disappointed I was watching your fine ass over here with him. No disrespect FAM" he said reaching his hand out to shake P-Funk hand.

"None taken I know she bad, he responded smacking her ass" Beast looked at the two confused

"I thought he was your brother" he asked

"Different mother brother she laughed, we just super close. He from VA too came down to check your club out I told him how dope it was. He's a big spender if you know what I mean"

"Ok well in that case, let me move you over to what we call the Baller Block. All the celebs that come through my city know about it! All the big money sits comfortably over there. I think you would prefer that section a lot better" he said directing them to the section. When they reached the section there were 5 nude women waiting for them and 2 bottles of Diplomatico Ambassador.

"Oh, so this how you make a nigga feel special" P-Funk said sitting next to Saucy one of the naked dancers.

"Yeah you go ahead of get comfortable I'm going steal Ms. Diamond away for a second if that's ok with you" Beast asked"

"Do your thing man! I'm going chill right here" he said smiling ear to ear. Beast lead Diamond into the back of the building where his office was. There was wall to wall to wall faux fur rug with leather Versace couches with faux fur throw blankets draped across the top. In the corner was huge fish tank with tropical fish and a marble waterfall. If his office screamed money, I can only imagine what his house looked like inside she thought.

"I see you like what you see" he said sitting down at his desk

"Yea it's alright", she joked

"Come closer you know you've been on my mind since I seen you. I wasn't sure I would even see you again. Then when I see you with dude it damn near broke my heart" he expressed

"Ha ha she laughed he's no threat. I knew I would be back to see your fine ass. So, what's your deal?" she asked sitting on his desk

"This is my deal baby I'm a business man handling my business"

"Well business man, she said spreading her legs in front of him. Where's your woman at tonight?" Beast was memorized by how pretty her pussy sat on the edge of his desk. She slowly licked her fingers and rubbed on it. Cat got your tongue babe" she asked seductively

"I'm waiting on you" he said. She bent down a placed her soft lips on his. One taste of her lips and he knew he needed more. He stuck his tongue deeper into her mouth as he rubbed on her exposed vagina. She unzipped his pants without unlocking their lips and pulled his 9-inch rock hard penis out of his pants. "I want you now" he whispered as he fingered her wet pussy while it dripped all over his desk. Beast lifted her off the desk and sat her face front slowly on his lap. She moaned with satisfaction as he entered her. He stroked as he lifted her slowly up and down his shaft. She winded her hips faster and faster while he moaned and bit her lip.

"You feel so good" he said

"You like that baby, bend me over" she moaned, Beast picked her up and bent her over his desk smacking he round plumped ass before entering her from behind. She thrust back as he grabbed her waist tighter. The 2 were interrupted by banging on the door. "Yo boss your mans is out here acting a damn fool he got to go" a voice yelled from the other end of the door. Beast pulled his pants up and walked towards the door. He checked to make sure she was covered before opening

"What's going on?"

"Old boy in the burgundy chink just knocked a nigga out for no reason! He's wired calling himself the king and shit. We were trying calm him down without fucking him up since he's in the VIP, but dude got to go real shit. Tonya caught ear of what the guy was saying. "I'll get him I apologize I'm the only one that can calm him down."

"Hold up baby I don't want this to mess up our night. I can have my guys handle your FAM" Beast said

"No, its fine Ill handle it and it won't trust me, I will get him situated and be back by closing if that's ok, she said kissing him. She ran as fast as she could to the VIP where P-Funk stood on the top of the mink couches screaming at the top of his lungs.

"Nigga she yelled grabbing him down what the fuck are you doing?"

"Oh, what's wrong babe shit I'm just living my best life this shits cracking" he said dancing around

"Did you lose track of why we here, get your shit together,"

"All part of the plan, he whispered pulling out his phone. He showed her a text from Diamond {I'm in let's get this money} She slightly smiled Now do your duty and get my drunk belligerent ass out of here"

Yeahh he yelled climbing back on the couch. Security began walking in their direction, but she waved them off

"I got him guys it's ok! Come on let's go get some fresh air maybe get you a cab or Uber" she said walking beside P-Funk stumbling body.

They reached the car in the parking lot P-Funk dove into the driver's seat

"So, what's the plan genius?" she asks sarcastically

"I am no longer your problem; I'll be around stay on task. Take your cute ass back in there and do your thing. Try to get him to take you to his crib that's where the money stashed. If not, we move to just duck taping and taking him there ourselves. I'm going play the background so won't anybody see me but when you leave the club I'll be right behind you. If for some reason you exit a different way shoot me a text. He is the jackpot baby so don fuck it up."

"I got you, I got us. I'm glad she made it in I knew she had it in her" she said before walking away. Funk drove out the parking lot and rode around the block a few times before entering the parking lot again, so he wouldn't look suspicious. He found a dim lit spot in the back where it was almost impossible to see anyone sitting in their cars while he waited.

"Back so soon, is old boy ok I should've known he wasn't built for this drink here" he joked

"Yeah he fine he gets so aggressive when he drinks! He just grabbed the car keys insisting he can drink whatever he's a grown man, so I let him go. I'll get a taxi or something later its fine"

"Girl your stuck with me you thought I was letting you get away from me twice especially after just a sample of the sweet kitty you're kidnapped"

"Kidnapped I don't know if I should be scared!" she joked

"Either way it's going feel good"

"Well if it feels and looks like the last place then a little scary won't hurt" she said reaching in to kiss him. He began to feel the erection in his pants, so he sat down.

"You know what have yourself a drink I'm going finish up early and we can head out if that's cool"

"Fine with me she said making her a drink" Beast disappeared back into his office Tonya texted Diamond {what's your status lil mama} and put her phone back in her purse and continued drinking. Beast sat in his office and watched her just to see if anything seemed fishy. He was concerned with who she kept checking her phone for but realized she was probably checking on P-Funk, so he thought nothing of it. Diamond responded {If only it was real} Tonya looked at her phone confused. Beast slowly approached her with his drink "everything ok" he asked she jumped nervously

"Oh yes you scared me, I was just trying to make sure he got home safe but of course his stubborn ass is doing just that being stubborn. I apologize again for him that's so embarrassing"

"No need we all have some sort of drama here or there. This may sound weird but what's your real name?

No offense but I deal with these women on a regular here and I understand what you do but I rather speak and address you on a more personal level if you don't mind he said. Tonya looked at him confused, from what she got and heard about this man he was exactly as his name says a Beast a monster but all he's been to her was generous and respectful. Could she be making a mistake she thought? Did I say something wrong?" he asked

"Oh no I'm sorry it just caught me off guard no one ever really cares to know my real name. Its Tonya!

"Tonya is pretty and it fits you better. I must sound cheesy, but I can see through you into your heart. Despite the things you may have done I can tell you're a good person and Diamond is a decoy to cover that. I won't get deep promise I just enjoy meeting people that surprise me and you Ms. Tonya are one of those people. How about we go chill in a hot Jacuzzi drink the finest liquor money can buy and really get physical with no interruptions"

"Well firstly thank you your words they mean more than you will ever know. This lifestyle can so easily be portrayed as who I really am instead of what and why I'm doing it. She said drinking her drink. I'm sorry I won't get too emotional but to answer your question yes I would love that right now" Beast grabbed her hand and lead her toward the back door. "Wait I see you got on them tall heels, go stand in the front Ill swing around and grab you so you won't have to walk these steps and risk falling" Tony stood in shock

"Ok and thank you that's so sweet" As she walked towards the door, she pulled her phone out and exited P-Funk {I think this is a mistake}

P-Funk saw the text as she was walking out of the club. He started his car in attempt to pick her up thinking she blew the entire mission when Beast pulled up from the side of the b building to pick her up. P-Funk responded {HANDLE YA FUCKIN BUSINESS} as he pulled off to follow a few cars behind.

Beast pulled up to the Spring Hills Suite on the North Shore. P-Funk wasn't far behind

"Is this where were going? She asked

"I mean yeah if that's ok with you? They have probably the hugest Jacuzzi tubs in the Burgh and the rooms are tight! I just want to enjoy you"

"No is fine I just thought I would be laid out on a bear skin rug naked in front of a fireplace or something after being in your office"

"I got you spoiled already huh, I don't live to far from here, he said as he was interrupted by his phone. Hello"

"Boss don't respond back to me act like you talking to somebody else" the voice said

"What now, one sec it's business" he said shaking his head

"So burgundy mink coat been following you this whole time, I know because I been following him. He never left the parking lot he just sat waiting on your and old girl to leave. I'm no genius but this looks like a setup.

"Mama Listen Ill stop past tomorrow I'm about to take my nice lady friend in for a comfortable Jacuzzi she been complaining about her back ok, so I'll see you tomorrow"

"Leave the info I'm bringing old boy in for a reunite let's get to the bottom of it"

"Bye Bye" Beast responded. Beast got out the car grabbing his things and went to Tonya's side to let her out.

"So, were staying then?"

"Yeah baby its nice trust me" The two walked into the hotel to check in. Tonya looked around confused wondering how the plan would still work. Beast gave all the information and the two proceeded to the room. The Jacuzzi was already full and bubbling along with drink lined on the outside.

"I see you're a regular" she joked

"Something like that" he responded

"Everything ok" she asked

"Yeah you here with me I'm great", Tonya instantly undressed and jumped in the Jacuzzi while Beast watched her. She rubbed the bubbles all over her exposed breast and blew kisses at him jokingly.

"Come on in with me I'm lonely" She whined when there was a knock on the door. Beast walked to the door to unlock it and P-Funk was pushed in and to the floor. Tonya jumped up "what's going on" she yelled

"Hmmm you tell me! Why is your brother following us huh? I thought he was so fucked up and not answering your calls"

"I don't know what you are getting at but why did your hurt him. What did he ever do to you?"

"Why! It looks like you two motherfuckers are trying to set me up" he yelled kicking P-funk in the stomach as he laid bruised and hurt on the floor.

"Set you up for what" she cried

"Don't try to play me. You're a stripper like the rest of them; I know you heard about me and who I am in this city. An you thought you two raggedy motherfuckers were just going take my money that easy"

"I never had any intentions on doing anything I thought you were a nice guy I just wanted to spend time with you she cried. Please don't hurt us it's not what you think!

"I don't trust nobody and I damn sure don't believe what you're saying so since I let you get a little bit closer than you probably should've you got to go"

"Go! What's that mean?" she cried. Diesel his security began screwing the silencer on the 35 he had on his left hip. You don't have to do this please" she yelled P-Funk laid on the floor half out of it not realizing what was going on.

"You all have a good night now I must get a comfortable nights rest" Beast said smiling before leaving the hotel

"Please don't do this I swear it wasn't what he thought she cried as the barrel of the gun pointed at the center of P-Funk head. The light flashed from the gun as Tonya watched P-Funk body go lifeless. She cried as the barrel was now pointed at her head. She wiped her tears looking him in his face "There's still a Diamond left motherfucker" she said before her body dropped lifeless into the Jacuzzi. Diesel pulled out the plastic wrap to dispose the bodies.

Chapter 18 (Every dog has its day) Ones strength is ones fuel always remember it's never your fault, but its

urgency that sometimes get you the best results
{AVENGE}

(4:32 am) Diamond sat on the floor of Beasts bedroom trying to reach P-Funk and Tonya but getting no response from neither. She began to panic realizing something was wrong. There were no signs that anyone was reading the text messages. She heard keys shaking at the front door downstairs. She cocked her gun and tip toed over to the banister to get a view of who was walking through the door. Beast drunkenly staggered in alone. She watched him from the corner of the steps as he punched in the alarm code dropping his keys on the kitchen floor.

"Motherfuckers thought they could rob me he said to himself pulling out the Yukon Jack pouring a drink. I'm Beast bitch now you and your lil nigga floating in the Allegheny River" he laughed as he downed his drink. Diamonds slowly backed up into the bedroom, she grabbed the towel full of broken glass and hid underneath the bed patiently waiting for him to come up the steps. Her heart raced nervously as she clinched the gun tight noticing her hands shaking. She laid as still as she possibly could as she held the gun face down to the floor. She could hear him mumbling but couldn't make out what he was saying. He yelled louder

"Bitch I need a moment to myself, I almost got killed tonight. Oh now you want to give me tears! Listen Mercedes I'm tired I'm drunk I'm about to lay down I'll call you when I get up take your ass to bed its 4 in the morning anyway call you tomorrow love you goodbye" he said before hanging up. Diamond trembled under the bed as she heard his foots steps on the steps getting closer to the bedroom. Beast entered the room turning on the TV; he sat on the bed and undressed. She could feel her breathing getting heavier as he kicked off his shoes dropping his pants to the floor. He walked pass her bag next to his bed into the bathroom. She hurried and grabbed her bag the minute she heard water running .Once she was sure he was in the shower she slid from underneath the bed with her gun pointed at the door. Her hands trembled as she walked closer; she noticed his gun on the night stand. She quietly removed all the bullets and left it on the stand. She pushed opened the door with the gun pointed in front of her, Beast stood naked in front of her with his head down and eyes closed as the water poured over his head. Rage rushed through her entire body as she watched him in silence. Everything in her wanted to just pull the trigger emptying the clip but that same rage knew she wanted to watch him die a slow and painful death. She backed up quietly sprinkling the broken glass along the doorway of the bathroom hoping that this plan would work. The room was dark besides the glare from the TV, so Diamond stood outside the bedroom door in the hallway and waited for him to finish.

Beast shut off the water, grabbing his towel he stepped out the shower. He rubbed the towel over his face and head as he walked into the bedroom. Without looking down he stepped into his bedroom planting both feet into the broken glass.

"Ahhh" he screamed as he fell to the floor. Diamond ran back into the bedroom grabbing his free hand as fast as she could while he was down, slammed it to the floor and drove her knife through the middle of his palm as hard as she could. The Hori blade broke through his hand and wedged into the floor. Beast screamed

"Big man screaming like a little girl, Shhhh I would hate to kill you right here right now she said standing over him with the silencer pointed directly at his face. Beast tried to focus on the voice he heard. Poor baby did that hurt? I hope so you fucking rapist! Remember me" Diamond said just hoping he would try something so she could shoot him.

"Diamond! He said in shock Why you doing this" he said sounding like he was in pain

"You know the more you move the more painful it gets. That called a Yo Hori Deba knife! Ouch I know that shit hurts" she laughed

Let's talk about this I didn't know a lot of things I know now!" he said

"How easy my name rolls off your tongue as if you know me! Like you raised me! Like you bought me so much as a fucking shirt to put on my back! Don't say my name again. You're nothing but a rapist! You took the only person I considered family!

"Mercedes don't care about you" he responded

"Mercedes! Fuck Mercedes that bitch can die slow for all I care I'm talking about Bam!"

"Bam! That aint your fucking family"

"SHUT THE FUCK UP! Don't even speak of his name! He was the closest thing to a father that I had and you took him from me" She yelled as tears rolled down her eyes. Beast tried to sit up but the blade continued to rip through his hand.

"Listen Bam felt sorry for you he did all that out of pity because of what he did to your mom!"

"My mom, that was his best friend stop lying," she yelled slapping him in the face "Listen, when you were a baby the only reason he even came around was because he thought you was his. He snuck and swabbed your mouth once your mom got killed because you were a product of rape a rape baby. He sent off the results and found out you were mine."

"Rape Baby so you raped my mother too!" she raised the gun at his head

"No! Look I won't talk bad on a dead man's name cause he aint here no more. He had mad love for your mom but a man's sexual attraction will always over power loyalty remember that. I made love to your mom that night, he on the other hand" he expressed trying not to rip into his hand anymore than it already was

"So what's that suppose to mean" she asked confused. Beast looked at her and laughed forgetting she's was so young.

"Look at you, he shook his head you're a baby this shit here aint your world. So what you plan to do kill me? I can't move my fucking hand I got blood coming from both ends like I'm fucking Jesus. What you really plan to do? If anything do it. Your hands is shaking you're scared shitless. I see you got the silencer so somebody gave you all the pointers you need to handle the job so what's it going be. I already became one with god baby girl so I'm ready to go either way"

"What the fuck did you mean about Bam and my momma?" she yelled

"He raped her! Shit let him tell it we both did; she was drunk out of her mind so we did what men do. She let me do it! So no it wasn't rape on my end! He talked all that best friend shit but the minute he got the chance guess what it went right out the window as I knew it would."

"You're lying" she replied

"Don't get wrong he loved her he even looked out for her matter fact he made sure he put you in the hall way before he slit her throat"

"Stop Lying! She yelled pulling the trigger of the gun shooting him in the shoulder. Beast screamed as his back hit the floor. Diamond paced back and forth unsure of what to do. She picked up her phone attempting to call P-funk again. "Where are you? Answer the phone Tonya please" she cried into the phone.

"Tonya, he said. It all makes sense now he groaned. So you were a part of this little stick up plan too. Well that shit aint go as plan I see. Where your back up" he laughed

"What"

"I smelled that dead rat from a mile away, now they both probably floating in the Allegheny River." Diamond stopped and looked at him. The more he laughed the more infuriated she became. She walked back over standing in front of him and shot out his knee caps. He screamed as he reached for her legs causing her to fall to the floor. She dropped the gun as he forcefully pulled her right leg toward him. She kicked as hard as she could as she tried to reach for the gun but it was too far out her reach.

"You little fucking bitch! He yelled now with his one free hand around her neck. Diamond kicked and swung as hard as she could but began to feel herself getting light headed. Just as she felt the calm of her body settle she noticed the big piece of glass lying on the floor next to her. She got hold of the glass and dug into his bleeding shoulder the bullet was still in. He screamed in agony releasing his grip from her neck. She crawled away as fast as she could and grabbed the gun. She turned around without thinking and shot 4 times. His body dropped to the floor. She crawled slowly to over to his stiff body and noticed all 4 bullets hit his chest. She sat on the floor next to him body unsure of what to do.

Diamond began searching the house for the money, she entered the guess room and looked in the spot the video showed but it wasn't there anymore. She searched all over the room and found nothing. She ram sacked the whole house and didn't find anything. She could hear his phone ringing from downstairs. It rang back to back to back, she looked at the id that read Cedes; she answered and didn't say anything.

"Hello! Hello" she yelled Diamond didn't respond is this a bitch! I know he aint laid up with some bitch answering his phone I'm on my way right fucking now stay there hoe" Mercedes yelled before hanging up. Diamond couldn't think of anywhere else to look but Beast had a fingerprint lock on his phone that had access to his alarm cameras. She ran upstairs tip toeing around his dead body to use his finger to unlock the phone. She opened the ADT alarm app and reviewed the footage. There was a safe underneath the living room glass table in the floor. "Jackpot" Diamond rushed down to the living room and attempted to push the heavy glass table over but it was too heavy. She found a hammer in the kitchen and shattered the glass all over the floor. She pulled the rug and floor board back that revealed the safe.

"Open the fucking door Beast" Mercedes yelled from the other end of the door. Diamond ran back upstairs to grab her gun. Mercedes continued to yell and bang on the door. Diamond peeked out to make sure she was alone. Unlocking the door she backed up with her gun pointed and waited for her to walk in.

"Where's the bitch! She yelled walking in the house when she was stopped by the gun

"Close the door" Diamond demanded, Mercedes looked surprised but did as she was told. Mercedes kept her hands up as she walked to the couch. There was glass everywhere and the house was trashed.

"Diamond what's going on and why are you here" she asked

"Hmm Why am I here" she sarcastically said standing in front of her you tell me Auntie! Why am I here?"

"I have no idea and why do you have a gun? What happened here" her eyes watered

"Get up let me show you something, she said pushing Mercedes towards the steps with her gun in her back. The two walked up the steps, Mercedes looked around as she slowly walked with tears running down her cheeks. She noticed Beast body lying on the floor in blood the before she reached the room. She screamed as she ran to his body "Baby get up she cried, baby"

"He's dead idiot" Diamond responded

"Diamond what the fuck is wrong with you why would you do this to him, where's his close why is he naked"

"Why! Why! Why! Again with these questions I know you know the answer to. Remember I used to wonder why and you never had a fucking answer for me I finally get it now! All this time since day 1 I never understood why you hated me so much. My mother's only sister my only family after pap died and you just turned your back on me and it was all for this piece of shit."

"Piece of shit you don't even know him! He was a good man" she yelled. Diamond slapped her across her face with the butt of the gun

"Get up! Let's go I know you know the code to that safe so let's go open it"

"I don't know the code to a damn safe"

"Listen Cedes my patience is running real thin and honestly where I'm at mentally right now I promise you if you don't open that safe expect your body to lie right next to his."

"All this over money what would you even do with it" she cried

"No all this over revenge the money is just a plus" she said following her back down the steps

"Revenge for what!" Mercedes yelled smacking Diamond across the face. Diamond kicked her in her stomach causing her to fall into the broken glass table.

"Revenge because he took everything from me! Revenge because he raped my mother and got her pregnant! Revenge because he watched her die she bleed out right in front of him while I laid in a freezing hallway with no clothes on! I was a baby his baby and he didn't even care. I was trash to him. He gave me a STD too I was bruised for days because he decided me his child a child was worth raping"

"Don't make up this shit to me" Mercedes yelled closing her ears. The look on her face as she cried Diamond knew she believed everything she was saying. "Oh my god, he touched the twin didn't he? Diamond asked. Mercedes cried harder, you know you're the worst then he could ever be open the fucking safe!" Diamond yelled angrily. Mercedes walked over to the safe and attempted to open it. She tried 3 separate times each time the code was wrong. Diamond walked up behind her and put the gun to the back of her head "A little motivation always helps" she said Mercedes tried again and still had no luck. Diamond cocked the gun. Mercedes tried again and it was incorrect, "Wait wait please don't shoot" she tried one last final time with sweat pouring down her face #05#15#2004 {beep beep} the safe sounded as it opened. Mercedes exhaled with relief but Diamond didn't remove the gun from the back of her head.

"It's open, take the money!" she yelled

"You know I never wanted anything more than to feel loved by you and your kids. You made my life so hard! Then you knowingly sat back while this man, my father your kids father fuck your daughter. Did you think I didn't I see the code? It was the twin's birthday that's some sick twisted shit. You are just as much of a rapist as him. "Diamond please don't do this" she cried. Diamond bowed her head and whispered to herself {Lord forgive me for my sins} BOW BOW she shot 2 times into the back of her head.

She dropped the gun on the floor and fell back on to the couch, tears began welling up. She could feel a lump in her throat as she fought back tears. She closed her eyes as the tears poured down her cheeks. So many emotions went through her body at once, the satisfaction of it being over but the reality that it's only just begun and she was all alone. She gathered herself together and went over to the safe. There were 3 duffle bags full of money, 2 guns a box of bullets and 2 sets of car keys. She took the car keys and went to the garage. Inside sat a Red Corvette with black 22-inch rims and an all-white Range Rover with 26 in rims.

She ran back up to the living room grabbed Mercedes keys hit the alarm looking out the front window to see what she was driving. A Blue Chevy Malibu nothing fancy or out of place. Diamond loaded each duffle bag into the trunk of the Malibu and went back into the house to take a shower. After she got dressed she exited the bathroom stepping over Beast lifeless body. She took one final look at him before leaving the house "Guess I'll see you in hell Daddy"

Chapter 19 (Close your eyes and put your ear to a seashell) don't let your sanity be disturbed find a median if the least. Let nothing or no one get in the way of your **{PEACE}**

Diamond got all the way to Arlington, MD without any suspicion while driving. She had one last stop before disappearing and nothing was stopping her from doing just that... She stopped at a Sheets gas station to fill up her tank and grab some food when she spotted a cop car pull up behind her parked car. She watched as they walked around the car checking to see if anyone was inside. Diamond ran into the bathroom and placed her ear to the door as she heard the bell go off signaling someone had walked in.

"Hey Bill, the cop said to the cashier. Who's driving the Malibu parked at pump 4? He asked Diamonds heart dropped unsure of what she should do. She couldn't leave the car, everything she owned was in that car.

"Oh it's just a young lady, average height light skinned looks like she's just passing through not from around here. Very pretty though she's in the restroom! Did you need her for something?"

"It a lady! Ok no problem we thought that Tibias made his way back around town from the Pa plates" the cop replied

"Oh no please don't speak him up, every time someone says his name here comes trouble" they all laughed.

"Alright well I'll leave you to it then," the cops said exiting the store. Diamond exhaled and walked back out the store. She grabbed her drink and chips and placed them on the counter as she watched the cops pull off.

"30 on pump 4" she said

"No problem and how are you today? He asked bagging her things

"I'm great!" she responded happy she could leave with no problems

"Well that's good to hear. Are you driving alone? Look like you're far from Pa"

"Yeah I'm only going about another 15 minutes and I got my road music so I'll be fine"

"Alright well buckle up drive safe there's loony tunes that drive crazy around here and thanks for visiting Maryland!'

"Thank you" she said leaving the gas station. As Diamond pumped her gas she couldn't help but feel a calming level of Peace. She reached in her bag in the trunk and walked back into the gas station. "Here you go; this is for your great customer service. I was having a bad day until now" she said handing him 500$. "

Why thank you ma'am" he generously responded

"No thank you! Stay positive its help more than you think" she walked out smiling got in her car and drove off. Diamond drove another 3 hours before reaching Virginia. It was already 10 o'clock so she knew it was too late to show up at the church. She called Tyrek

"Are you ok?" He answered paranoid

"Wow I didn't think you cared" she laughed

"Quit playing seriously though I was worried I'm glad you're ok"

"Of course I'm ok relax"

"So did you do everything you needed to do?"

"As a matter of fact I did"

"So what's in store for you now? Are you thinking about just staying in Pittsburgh?"

"Actually I'm starving and was wondering if you wanted to join me"

"What you mean"

"Look outside" she replied. Tyrek walked out the house smiling ear to ear happy to see her.

"Girl what you doing driving?" he asked hoping in the car

"I'm realizing there's not too much that I can't do these days" she joked

"Damn Diamond look at your neck and your lip are you hurt" he asked sincerely

"Hurt wow that's a great word to use, she said I am but I'm fighting through it I'm a big girl"

"We don't have to talk about it, scoot your ass over you is not driving me around with your young ass. Let's go get your belly full you're hungry right?

"Yeah I can eat" she responded

"Good I got the perfect place for you" he said hopping in the driver seat.

Tyrek pulled up and Diamond instantly start laughing

"What's so funny" he laughed back

"Seriously McDonalds again" she yelled

"Girl get your little boujie butt out the car we eating Mickey Dees"

The 2 walked in ordered there food then sat at the same booth from the first time they met there. Diamond laughed with him as she ate her food completely freeing herself from her mind and it felt great.

"I still can't believe you drove here from Pittsburgh! What did you come back here for anyway? I thought you would have disappeared."

"Yeah I plan to but I had to handle something important here so I came back" she said looking him in his eyes. He noticed how she was looking at him and looked down trying to avoid contact.

"Oh yeah what's that"

"What's what" she asked

"The important business here"

"Well..."

"Diamond look before you even say it I'm flattered and I aint going lie I like you too I really do but we would never work I'm like 8 years older than you. No one would go for that. I have to block anything but friendship with you out my head as hard as it may be" he said not lifting up his head. Diamond looked at him confused

"Wait is you saying you like me Tyrek?" she asked

"It's pretty evident I thought! I'm sorry if I lead you on I'm assuming that's why you came back right for me?"

"Actually no it wasn't, I mean I like you as my friend you were really good to me but I knew you were too old for me I didn't even think you thought I was pretty let alone liked me."

"Pretty Diamond you're gorgeous smart and fearless. I'm not trying to come off like no creep but when you get older I hope you keep me in mind. I would love to take you out on a real date one day not McDonalds!" he laughed feeling embarrassed. Diamond walked over to the booth he was sitting in and gave him a hug for what seemed like forever. Then planted a kiss on his cheek

"Thank you Tyrek and I promise I plan to find you down the road so you can take me to something way nicer than this like Taco Bell" she joked breaking the awkwardness between the two. They finished up there food and Tyrek drove himself back to his house.

"But seriously though, why you come back? Please don't tell me to do something to old ass Tauti"

"No please she's dead to me, I honestly came back to speak to your dad"

"My dad! Talk to him about what!"

"I don't think you would understand so I rather not go into detail. Is he home?"

"No not right now he's out with my mom more than likely it won't be until late that he comes home but he got service in the morning."

"That's cool Ill find somewhere to park and sleep and just come to service in the morning."

"You were going sleep in your car?"

"Uh it's not like I have some mansion to go sleep in"

"Why won't you go back to P-funks Place?"

"I thought we weren't going to talk about it"

"We don't have to I just want to make sure your not sleeping in your car!"

"I'll be fine" she replied

"No you won't, come on. You can stay in one of the guest rooms"

"Is that a good idea?" she asked hesitantly
"Won't anybody even know you're there. When you get up

everybody will be gone you can just leave out it's no problem trust me" Diamond took his word locked up the car and went into the house.

Tyrek got her set up in the guest room on the bottom floor away from everyone. Tory was at an aunts house so the house was completely empty. He got her a towel and wash cloth, scissors, comb and hairbrush "Have a good night, if I don't see you before you leave be safe and good luck to you.

"Thank you Tyrek you don't know how much this means to me I truly appreciate you" He smiled before attempting to close the door behind him. Diamond put her foot in the doorway stopping the door from shutting. Tyrek looked back at Diamond confused. She slowly walked close to him placing her arms around his neck and deeply kissing him. At first he hesitated then began to kiss her back. He pushed her back into the room seductively kissing her and palming her ass. He laid her on the bed as he kissed her neck, while she laid back with her eyes closed in ecstasy. Diamond reached from his belt but Tyrek stopped her.

"Good night Diamond, he said exiting the room. Diamond sat up smiling in satisfaction. Tyrek gave her that tingling feeling in between her legs and she wanted so bad to explore it. Diamond walked over to the mirror and looked at herself, although she still seen the innocent girl with the baby face, big sandy curls and brown eyes deep down she knew that girl was gone forever. Grabbing handfuls of her hair she began to cut and cut slowly massaging jet black dye through her hair and across her eyebrows. She sat in the shower as the water beat upon her back watching as the black dye went down the drain realizing that's what her heart slowly became Black.

The next morning

Diamond pulled up to the church about 840 a.m. The first service wasn't starting until 9 so she made good timing. Sister Johnson was sitting in the pulpit going over paperwork while Tory sat 3 rows back reading her bible and humming a hymn. Diamond quietly sat next to her. 'Hey" she said. Tory looked at her like a stranger

"Diamond I almost didn't recognize you! Look at your hair is everything ok?"

"For the first time in a long time yes its better than ok. Where's your dad at?" she asked

"He's in the back getting ready for service, did you" Diamond got up and walked away mid sentence of Tory talking. She peeked in to make sure the he was alone. He sat at his desk highlighting scripts from the bible. Tory watched Diamond unsure of what she could've wanted with her father.

"Pastor" she interrupted opening his door.

"Yes can I help you, he said focusing his attention on who was at the door. Well I'll be! He said in astonishment. Now that's something different! Do you feel different? I'm going to answer that for you and say yes only because you came back. You look hurt are you hurt? Sit down Sit down" he said guiding her to a chair

"Thank you Pastor, I do feel different but I don't know if it's a good different bad different or just indifferent" she said with her head down. I brought something for you and please don't tell me you can't or won't take it because I came all the way back here to give this to you."

"What's this he said looking in the bag?

"Its 60,000 dollars and I want you to have it" she mumbled without putting her head up.
"Diamond look at me! Look at me! Diamond wouldn't put her head up. Why are you giving me this money and where did it come from? She began to cry. You poor girl what trouble are you in? Let me help you!" Diamond wiped her eyes and lifted her head

"I apologize for what my original thoughts of you were. I knew about you and Tauti I knew you were cheating on Sister Johnson and it angered me. I didn't respect you for that I despised you for that. I stole from your church because I had a plan to kill my father for killing my mother. For killing the only man that would ever love me like a father and taking my innocence and throwing me away like garbage." Pastor Johnson stood heartbroken wiping away her tears and I did what I had to do to him along with 3 other people throughout my time on this earth, she said pulling out the gun and placing it on his desk. I'm telling you all of this because I enjoyed every minute of it! Those who bring me hurt or pain I will avenge every time and they will feel my raft eventually Pastor.

Now I plan to never mention this again in life but I'm also giving you the opportunity to again call the cops and put me away." Diamond stood transparent in the Pastors eyes, he could truly feel everything she was feeling at that moment.

"Diamond I want to help you what good would you do in jail? You need someone to show you it's ok to love and be loved back without disappointment. Everyone isn't out to hurt you child"

"You know I love to write, I wanted to be a writer one day. I was a happy child even though everything around me put blood sweat and tears into ruining me. I love your son Tyrek she said wiping her eyes. I became good at reading people and he has a pure and sincere soul it's refreshing and something I needed to feel before I completely broke. And I love you pastor because I seen that same purity when you let me walk out of your church knowing I was stealing for you."

"We all got a story Diamond cant nobody judge you but god" he said

"You knew your speech wouldn't help me you knew I would still do exactly what I wanted you read me didn't you? Now how does that work exactly pastor?" she said

"God knows all his children. God knows your heart Diamond"

"Don't stop being a good person and spreading that word no matter how unbelievable it may seem I know you mean well. You won't see me again after today! All my hurt frustration fear disappointment resentment and any other emotion controlled by someone else actions is gone. The sweet Diamond I once knew is gone and now I'm going to move on and find out exactly who this new Diamond is. I just had to stop and show my gratitude and pay you back. Thanks for everything and please continue to pray for me" She said walking out of the office.

"Diamond! Diamond!" Pastor Johnson yelled as Diamond kept walking exiting the church, the pastor let her go.

"Yo! Tyrek yelled grabbing Diamonds attention what was all that about with my dad in there I seen you in his office?"

"Let's just say I owed him! Tyrek thank you for everything and I mean everything! You're a great person and I will always remember you"

"I'm guessing you leaving for good this time huh, hence your hair and things" he joked

"Yeah I think it's time I keep it moving leaving the past in the past but keep your number the same never know when I might pop up" she said starting her car

"You do know you're driving illegal even though your little Rihanna haircut gives you a few years you still wet behind the ears young buck. The 2 laughed Whelp I'll see you around he said kissing her forehead. He paused for a second then proceed to connect his lips to hers kissing her soft and passionately. Diamond smiled and pulled off with no destination but she was rich and that's was enough for her.

She stopped at the corner store passing Woodbridge to fill up her tank and grab some snacks for her long ride to nowhere. She put in her order for her steak hoagie and fries. As she waited 2 guys entered the gas station one was on the phone yelling.

"Bitch! Do I look like I give a fuck! I'm Bonez deal with it or find another nigga that do you this good." He yelled hanging up. The name Bonez seemed so familiar to her. As she waited for her food she tried to remember exactly where she remembered that name from. Tonya! She thought. The vision of her at the front door bleeding and bruised quickly triggered her. She wanted to just get her food get in her car and pull off but she knew she owed it to Tonya. "Excuse me sir, did I hear you say your name was Bonez?"

"Who you?" he asked she smiled

"Oh I don't think you know me but I remember my Auntie Diamond mentioned you. I thought you died!

"Died, he laughed yall hear this little bitch. Call me Jesus baby cause as you can see I didn't" he said

Yeah I see that. My Auntie Diamond used to talk about you. I thought maybe you guys used to date I'm sorry my mistake" she said turning around. Number 24 the cashier yelled out implying Diamonds food was done.

"Diamond, oh you mean that stripping ass bitch! We didn't date we fucked over and over. Matter of facts where that bitch at?" he said walking up behind Diamond aggressively

"Honestly I don't know it's been awhile but if you see her tell her everything's going to be alright. I got everything she'll know what it means" Diamond said walking out the store. Bonez watched her walk out brushing her off. Diamond got in her car reaching into her backseat pulling out the pink duffle bag that held her 40 Caliber fully loaded. She took a look at herself in the rear view mirror cocked her gun back.

"Well it looks like I didn't retire just yet. One more stop won't hurt" she grinned

TO BE CONTINUED

299

Made in the USA
Lexington, KY
14 September 2019